Vipasha

In amethi,

Rahim

Mari

EASTERINE KIRE

HarperCollins *Publishers* India
a joint venture with

New Delhi

First published in India in 2010 by
HarperCollins *Publishers* India
a joint venture with
The India Today Group

Copyright © Easterine Kire Iralu 2010

ISBN: 978-93-5029-018-7

2 4 6 8 10 9 7 5 3 1

HarperCollins *Publishers*
A-53, Sector 57, NOIDA, Uttar Pradesh – 201301, India
77-85 Fulham Palace Road, London W6 8JB, United Kingdom
Hazelton Lanes, 55 Avenue Road, Suite 2900, Toronto, Ontario M5R 3L2
and 1995 Markham Road, Scarborough, Ontario M1B 5M8, Canada
25 Ryde Road, Pymble, Sydney, NSW 2073, Australia
31 View Road, Glenfield, Auckland 10, New Zealand
10 East 53rd Street, New York NY 10022, USA

Typeset in 10.5/14 Sabon
Jojy Philip New Delhi 110 015

Printed and bound at
Thomson Press (India) Ltd

*To Mari, Uncle Sam, Azuo Zhabu, Marina
and Mama and JJ*

Author's Note

Mari, or Khrielieviü Mari O'Leary, is my mother's eldest sister and this is her story. My mother is the youngest of four siblings. Samuel, the oldest, was the only son of my grandparents. He was followed a few years later by Mari, then came Zhabu, the second daughter, and last of all, Mama. The four of them were separated from their parents during the Japanese invasion of India via the Naga Hills in 1944. Finally reunited at the end of the war, this is their story too.

I started writing *Mari* when I was about sixteen. I wrote it in my head during my summer holidays with Mari in northern Assam, listening to her tell this story and badgering her to tell it again and again. I always knew I would write it down one day. I finally wrote it in 2003, with the help of Mari and a diary she had kept during the war years. It took several interviews and long-distance phone calls to get the missing details from both Mama and Mari, the two sisters left of the four siblings. What I had in 2003 was skeletal. Much time has been spent since then, trying to flesh it out with more details that dear Mari goes over with me patiently. I must have read the diary a hundred times and still I cry a little at certain parts.

For Mari and the others of her generation, World War II and the Japanese invasion of our lands was the most momentous period of their lives. Everything happened at the same time. Growing up, falling in love, war, homelessness, starvation, death and parting and, finally, peace. All my oral narrators told me this about the war: 'It altered our lives completely.'

What is so remarkable about World War II, which is still referred to as *The War* by the Nagas, is that people have very little memory of what they were doing before the war years. I was left with the impression that the war, for us, was almost equivalent to the big bang, the beginning of all life.

When they recounted their war experiences, even ninety-year-olds came to life. Eyes glowing with excitement, one of my narrators told me, 'The first time I ever saw an aeroplane was during the war. I had heard people talk about them but I had never seen one before. I stood there and looked at it and cried out, "Oh, to think that we were to see this in our lifetime!"'

The pre-war town of Kohima has been recreated mostly through Mama's and Mari's eyes. They told me about landmarks in the town such as the shops and the school and the hospital. They remembered the gallows used during British times to hang murderers, the pillory set up to deter wrongdoers from repeating their offence, the names of their teachers and the number of cars in town. It was as though an entire lost era was unfolding slowly before my eyes.

The town of Kohima was originally an outpost of the village of Kohima, consisting of government offices and residences. When the missionaries and the Indian businessmen and the British administrators came into the picture, the locals called the small township Tephriera, or Indian village.

In the early forties, there were just two cars in town. In fact, the population was so small that there were only two schools: an Assamese school and the Mission School, which ran classes I to VI. Those who wanted to study further went to Shillong to complete their matriculation.

Reminiscing about the war years is very common with a certain generation in Kohima. Those of us who never knew the war feel as though we have missed out on a life-changing event. Indeed, it was such for those who lived through it for Kohima was never the same again.

Development had come rapidly with the building of the roads. A great number of new roads were built during the war. The Naga freedom struggle that followed upon the heels of the war cast a dark shadow over our lands. In retrospect, there are many who continue to see the war years as the best years of their lives. It has been that romanticized. Grim? Certainly. But they were years filled with all the elements of romance: heroic deeds, the loss of lives, fear, uncertainty and deep love. These are all part of Mari's story.

In 1974, Mari's father lost his lands. In a giant landslide, Grandfather's house and orchard and Grandmother's gardens were all taken away. Both my grandparents were dead by then.

The house that Mari grew up in no longer stands. Memories are all that remain.

THE BATTLE OF KOHIMA

It is hard to imagine present-day Kohima as the site of the most decisive battlefield of the Burma Campaign. Never as famous as the storming of Normandy or the siege of Tobruk, the Battle of Kohima came to be called 'the forgotten battle' and its veterans the 'forgotten heroes'. This was the first British victory over the Japanese, and the first stop on their journey eastwards and towards Japan's final surrender. War historians who became aware of its significance have called the battle the 'Stalingrad of the East'. It was fought from 4 April to 22 June 1944.

Footprints and horse droppings and movement in the forests had long confirmed to the villagers that the Japanese had entered their territory. But it was on the fourth of April, the fourth month in 1944, at 4 p.m. that they finally revealed themselves. They rapidly occupied the villages to the south of Kohima and began to fire on targets in Kohima.

Codenamed Operation U-GO, the Japanese plan was originally to disrupt the Allied offensive plans for that year. The Japanese army had so far had spectacular conquests: against the Dutch West Indies and the Philippines, against mainland Asia and Oceania. When Singapore fell, the British forces suffered their biggest blow in south-east Asia. The Burma road, so vital for supplies to China, was in great danger of being closed down by the Japanese. As feared, the road was soon cut off and China became isolated, resulting in terrible losses for the Chinese army and even worse losses for Chinese civilians. By March and April 1942, Japan had completely overrun Burma and British and Indian contingents were forced westward over the river Chindwin.

The Japanese commander, General Renya Mutaguchi of the Japanese 15th Army, expanded the original plan and decided to invade India and attempt to overthrow the British Raj. With the British army in retreat, part of the plan involved sending the 30,000-strong Japanese 31st Division to capture Kohima and cut off Imphal. The Japanese 31st Division's commander, Lieutenant General Kotoku Sato, had misgivings about Mutaguchi's plan. He expressed fear that they might starve to death on the expedition.

General William Slim, commanding the 14th Army, was preparing to establish a defensive line at Imphal. He was not expecting an attack on Kohima as there was no road leading there from Burma. Slim chose Imphal to fight upon because the Imphal plain was the only suitable place for an airfield over thousands of kilometres of some of the roughest terrain.

The fiercest fighting took place during the siege of Kohima, which began on 6 April, and lasted until reinforcements, in the form of British 2nd Division's 5 Brigade and 6 Brigade, arrived on 19 April. The besieged Kohima garrison was composed of an assorted group of both combatants and non-combatants of about 2,500. Colonel Hugh Richards, who had earlier served with the Chindits, was in charge of the garrison. The numbers defending Kohima were made up by the Assam Regiment, one battalion of the Indian 161st Infantry Brigade, the Queen's own Royal West Kent Regiment, the Shere Regiment (of the Royal Nepalese Army) and some companies of the Burma Regiment. Highly outnumbered, the Kohima garrison received help from the local Nagas who acted as scouts, spies, stretcher-bearers and ammunition carriers to assist the Allied troops in uprooting the Japanese invasion. It was a crucial battle. Not surprisingly, one of the books written about this strategic battle was titled *Springboard to Victory*. The book, written by Lucas Phillips, gives a detailed account of the siege of Kohima and the tenacity with which its defenders ousted the Japanese army.

Even after winning the 'battle of the tennis court' (which was fought for about two weeks around the district commissioner's tennis court), the Allied forces fought for another two months to force out Japanese troops from the northern Angami villages and to the east of Kohima. By this time, the monsoons had set in and the terrain had turned muddy, making movement and supply of rations very difficult. The Japanese had stubbornly dug into Kohima village and Aradura Spur. After 16 May, these two areas were finally taken over by the British troops.

A major factor in the repulsion of the Japanese invasion was the lack of supplies. The three-week quota of rations that 31 Division travelled with was not replenished except with what they could extort from villages. In the three-month battle, the British and Indian forces lost 4,000 men, including those who died and those who went missing. The Japanese forces lost 5,000 men, and many more died of disease and starvation on their way back. The battle was to go down in history as one of the greatest battles noted for its 'naked unparalleled heroism' as Lord Mountbatten called it. After the battle, Mountbatten wrote to the troops: 'Only those who have seen the horrific nature of the country under these conditions will be able to appreciate your achievements.'

Mari is not just Mari's story. It is the story of Kohima and its people.

Kohima today is very different from the Kohima of my childhood, and completely unrecognizable from the Kohima of Mari's childhood. Crowded sidewalks. Ugly gaping holes in the landscape where the unstable land has slipped away. Jostling people on busy streets where only the terror of a sudden bullet flying to its target can temporarily disperse the masses. Old houses leaning against new concrete shopping malls. And faces, people's faces, always anxious, fearful and hardened by the toil of surviving.

Above the din of traffic, the war cemetery rises with its green terraces and carefully planted flower beds. Like a monument of a nobler time. The fallen sleep there, their epitaphs still bringing tears to visitors' eyes. Once upon a time, a war was fought here and it changed lives. The lives of those who died. And those who lived, whose loved ones never returned, the ones who had to find within themselves the strength and courage to rebuild, to forgive, to love and to celebrate life again.

EASTERINE KIRE

When you go home
tell them of us
and say for your tomorrow
we gave our today.

Inscription on the war memorial of the
2nd Division at the Kohima War Cemetery

Prologue

Kohima. It is dusk now. I can hear the cicada's plaintive cries. The birds have stopped their chirping and there is silence all around. My window overlooks the woods below our house. The orange glow of the setting sun is subdued, the grey of twilight quickly overtaking it. The silhouettes of the hills and the neighbourhood houses are sharp in this half-light.

Kohima's myriad houses cover every hillock and its roads wind themselves around the hills, and the lights that come on at dusk are like bright little splashes dispelling the dark. My house on Bayavu Hill is still close enough to the woods to allow me to hear the sounds of the birds and insects. I am constantly aware that this may not last much longer, considering how quickly people are building houses everywhere around me.

This is the loneliest time of my day, this hour of closure when daytime sounds recede and memories crowd in like moths to a flame. Memories that mingle joy and grief, light and darkness. More on some days and less on others. More today because I spent all afternoon cleaning the attic and found my diary. I thought I had lost it. I found it tucked away between sheaves of old newspapers and magazines. I carefully pulled it out and rubbed off the dust with the end of my apron. Not one page was missing.

Around me lie books on the war. I have bought every book on the Burma Campaign that I could find. Only we who have seen the war feel this way. We relive it again and again.

I open the diary slowly. The childish scrawl of a young girl fills its pages and, as I read on, I am almost that girl again. Carefree and innocent and oblivious to the way in which the war would change my life forever. I am drawn once again, irresistibly, into that mad whirl of living, loving and dying. That was the war I knew.

I had thought then that life began at seventeen. And that life began in spring. I was seventeen that spring when I met Victor. And the world was green with the young green of new plants, the hills bathed with thin mist every evening and the nights velvet with the songs of Bing Crosby. It was the spring of 1943. How little I knew of life then. How very different Kohima was.

February 1943

I FEBRUARY

It's a new year now. I am sitting by my bedroom window, my diary propped up on the little table, the blank pages dimly lit by my kerosene lamp. My thoughts are full of the year that has passed. So much has happened. I hope I can remember to write all of it down.

1942 was a year of countless rumours about a great war that was sweeping over the lands east of us. People had begun to speak of it with great interest, of the fierce armies of Japan marching across south-east Asia. Just before Christmas 1941, news of the bombing of Pearl Harbour had reached us on the radio. The men talked about how the war in Europe was engulfing the whole world. They said the war was likely to push into India next. But we lived in such a remote part of the world that we didn't really think we would be touched by the war. Life was still fairly normal for us in 1942.

Our little town was the headquarters for the British administrative office in the Naga Hills. Our hills lay on the border of India and Burma, part of Assam.

Most people lived in Kohima village with houses on the hilltops. On the outskirts of the village were the Mission Compound and the Choto Bosti colony. The new colonies that were developing included the Public Works Department colonies, which served as government quarters for the Indians who worked in the district commissioner's office. The town, which lay in the valley below, was full of shops and Manipuri hawkers' stalls. Further on was the district commissioner's office where Father worked.

We lived on the slope above the town, in the colony known simply as Mission Compound. There were seven of us: Father and Mother, my foster sister Marina, my brother Samuel and my sisters Zhabu and Aneiü. Sam was twenty-three then, and had recently married Bano. They were expecting their first baby. My sister-in-law Bano was an educated young woman. She was an excellent weaver and could weave very fast. She used to weave beautiful waist-cloths and body-cloths for us those days.

My brother was a mild-mannered man. He was always a little serious and took over his family responsibilities early. Though he had the duties of a married man, he still made time for us, his sisters, and tried to help us in whatever way he could. The two younger girls, Zhabu and Aneiü, kept each other company. Zhabu was closer to me in age and we could talk about girlish things. We did many things together: going to the fields on holidays or gathering herbs in the forest. We even had the same group of friends. Aneiü, eleven years old, liked to play house and she would persuade Zhabu to play with her. When our cousins visited, they played together all day long, running in and out of the house constantly.

Marina was a little younger than Sam. She had been with

us since she was seven. Her father was a Khasi, a native of Meghalaya, and her mother Angami.

'What a good worker Marina is!' Anyie Kereikieü, our aunt, remarked one day when she came to visit.

Mother smiled and replied, 'Yes, she is a quick learner. She is a better weaver than I am now.'

'She looks so much like you. You could be mistaken for her mother,' Anyie said. This was true. Even though she was not a blood relation, Marina was the one who resembled Mother the most. In her gestures, in her gentle manner of speaking and even in the way she looked, she was so like Mother, so much so that strangers would often mistake them for one another.

Mother was very proud of her and would always praise her: 'Marina can read the Bible and she has a beautiful singing voice. She is such a good cook, too. Any man who marries her will be fortunate.' Marina would blush and go off to do some work in the garden. But I don't think I was ever jealous of the way Mother praised Marina. It never occurred to me to be jealous. We all loved Marina dearly.

Anyie lived in Kohima village. She and our other relatives would visit us all the time, bringing news of happenings in the village. 'It's a genna day today,' she announced that day.

'Is it a fire genna day or a water genna day?' Mother asked her. The genna days were no-work days when it was taboo to work in the fields or woods. They were very important in the old religion.

'A fire genna,' Anyie replied. 'It is taboo to light a fire in the fields today so as to prevent drought in the year to come.' Though we were Christian, we abided by these cultural practices in order to live in harmony with the non-Christians.

Anyie Kereikieü was not Christian. She was Father's
cousin, so we called her Anyie, which meant paternal aunt.
We were a little frightened of her, because she would not
hesitate to perform her duty of scolding us if she thought
our work was shoddy.

'How old is Aviü now?' she asked my mother, turning her
attention to me suddenly. I was cleaning rice in a winnowing
mat, and hoped she wouldn't notice that I hadn't tied a
scarf around my head like she always told us to do.

'She turned sixteen last month,' Mother replied.

Anyie looked at me again and said, 'Hmm, at her age, I
was already married and a mother of one.'

'Times have changed, Akieü,' said Mother mildly.
'The children want to be educated before they think of
marriage.'

'Yes,' Anyie agreed, but I knew that deep down she
thought that educating girls was a waste of time, as did most
of the non-Christians. In the Naga culture, the woman's
role was to look after the house and children, and nothing
beyond that.

Anyie told us that the people in the village were anxious.
'The men are talking about a war in the east. People can't
stop talking about the Japanese and some are afraid that
they might enter our lands.'

'Is that possible?' Mother whispered, almost to herself.
But we knew more about these developments than Anyie
did. Father listened to the radio every night and told us all
the world news.

'Esh! I don't believe it,' Anyie continued. 'The white man's
government is too powerful to let that happen. Remember
how hard our clansmen fought the British when they first
came? Our best warriors fought the white man. We even

had help from warriors from Khonoma. And still we were crushed. The Japanese are coming from so far, how can they defeat the British when our own men couldn't?'

In a way, Anyie mirrored what most of our people, educated or non-educated, thought. We didn't see the war as any great danger to us. Everyone knew there was a war going on in Europe but it seemed a distant thing for us here, in our corner of the world. Father, naturally, was extremely curious about everything to do with the war and turned on his radio every morning and night for updates.

'The Japanese have bombed Pearl Harbour!' he had announced just before Christmas 1941. Father told us about the developments that could follow such a bombing. So we knew more about the progress of the war than people like Anyie who did not have a radio.

As an officer in the treasury, Father looked after all the confidential papers. He worked directly under Charles Pawsey, the district commissioner, who lived in the official district commissioner's residence below Garrison Hill, in a very pretty house with a tennis court in the front yard. The house faced east and had a panoramic view of Kohima village and the villages to the north and east. Mr Pawsey lived alone in that big house. He was a strict man, held in awe by his subordinates. In most respects, I suppose he could be seen as the mayor of Kohima. Everyone called him the DC.

2 FEBRUARY

On Saturdays, we had no school. That was the day we washed our clothes. We also went to town that day, which was something we always looked forward to. Zhabu and I never stayed out for long if we went on our own, but Aneiü always wanted to come with us and then we would have to wait for her to finish looking at all the shops, and we invariably reached home late.

What an odd thing I have just remembered. It's about the day Mother sent me with Aneiü to buy tea and lentils. We took the path from our house down to Mission Road. From there, we were walking towards the main road when we saw a crowd of people. They were standing outside the police station.

'What a lot of people,' said Aneiü curiously. 'What do you think they are doing?'

I stood on my toes and tried to look above the heads of the crowd but I couldn't see what was going on. Aneiü let go of my hand and ran into the crowd. I hurried after her.

The crowd was mostly made up of men, but there were a few women and children, too. We looked over the heads of the children and were shocked at what we saw. A prisoner was being put in the stocks and everyone was watching because he was struggling so hard. He was a big man and he snarled and cursed when they shoved his head in the opening and locked it. The holes for his arms were too small for his large hands, which were roughly thrust through them. Defiantly, he rolled his eyes and looked at the crowd. For a few moments, his dark eyes turned to me and he stared at me.

'Aviü!' Aneiü whispered nervously and clutched my hand tightly. I tore my gaze away from the man and we turned quickly and walked away as fast as we could. 'Aviü, he was looking straight at you!' Aneiü exclaimed. I didn't reply but I was terrified. I held onto her hand and walked faster, trying to calm down. There was no way he could come after me but we kept walking until we reached the shops, not daring to look behind us.

'Why was he put in the stocks?' Aneiü asked after a while. 'Do you think he was brawling?"

'He must have been arrested for drunkenness, he still looked drunk!' I answered. Men caught drunk and brawling were the ones who ended up there. The stocks were set up just below the police station, in full view of the main road. But the man we had seen looked so hardened, he couldn't be just a drunk, I thought.

'He looked like a really bad man,' said Aneiü. I didn't tell her I thought he looked like a murderer. Criminal laws were very harsh under the British government. Thieves were sent to Tezpur to serve long sentences. Murderers were hanged in Kohima itself. None of us had seen the gallows that were put up towards Aradura, far away from the town.

'Let's not stop to watch next time,' I said to Aneiü. 'I don't want them to see our faces.' She nodded. We were both quite shaken when we entered the shop where we were to buy our groceries.

The shop smells made us forget what had just happened. Duosao dukan or 'Duosao's shop' always smelt of a mixture of things – soap, Indian spices and the cloying fragrance of sugar – when we stood next to the jute bags in which they were stored. We bought a kilo of tea and some lentils. We giggled a little at the Marwari shopkeeper's funny accent when he spoke to us in Tenyidie, our native language. The local people had named him Duosao, no one knew his real name. All the Marwaris spoke our highly tonal language flatly, with no stresses. The boys at school would imitate them and make everyone laugh.

When we came out of the shop, Aneiü's attention was drawn to the flowers that were blooming all over town. 'Look at that!' she exclaimed in delight, pointing at the daisies and petunias blooming in-between the houses.

Flowers grew wild all over town because there were such few houses. Here and there grew flowering trees like the pink bohemia and the scarlet flame of the forest. The town certainly looked colourful with the trees and flowers all around. We found rhododendrons on Aradura Hill but not on the lower slopes closer to town. Aneiü wanted to pick daisies so we stopped for a while. When we were done, we bought eggs from the Manipuri hawkers because Mother had told us to buy the eggs at the very end. The Manipuris were popular with the local people. They sold dried fish and small yeast-balls which the non-Christians bought to make rice beer.

We got home earlier than usual that day. The memory of that man in stocks still sent shivers through me and when we were in the house, we told the others about him. Mother was sitting on the floor, weaving with Marina. They were both a little shocked but said they had seen people like that before. Aneiü and I made tea for them both and since it was still early, I polished the floors with wax.

5 FEBRUARY

When I close my eyes, I can still picture my house; I can see it clearly. I know every nook and corner so well. The three wide bedrooms downstairs, a well-used sitting room and a large kitchen.

The rooms upstairs were sometimes occupied by visiting relatives. In one of the rooms, we stored heavy wooden and tin trunks filled with clothes. One of the trunks contained Mother's old dresses, lovely poplins that we would try on now and then. We also stored stacks of magazines with pictures of the royal family and movie stars. Mother and Marina often sat upstairs and wove waist-cloths and body-cloths.

But in the evenings, those rooms sent shivers down my spine. There was a musty smell in there that we never seemed to get rid of, no matter how many times we aired the rooms. At night and on afternoons when I was alone in the house, I sometimes heard the creaking of footsteps on the floors above, a heavy tread that left me breathless with fear. Once, when a cousin came to visit, he slept in one of the rooms and the next morning he claimed to have seen the ghost of an old woman. Mother shushed us when we talked about it and told us there were no such things as ghosts. Still, amongst ourselves, we could never resist talking about the upstairs rooms and the beings that might be inhabiting them. Mother was the bravest person I knew. She stayed all alone in that house throughout the war. But that came much later.

Our house had been built on a slope. On the land above the house, Father dug terraces where we grew herbs. Our land stretched downward for about fifty metres till it reached Mission Road.

At the entrance to our house was a thick bamboo grove, so thick in parts that you couldn't see beyond it to the town below. It gave our house its name – Bamboo Villa. Beyond the bamboo grove was a small stream with a bridge over it; it was very pretty, really. The stream never dried up, not even in winter, and the water would overflow after a heavy downpour and the muddy water would rush down in torrents. The bridge was about ten feet long and had iron girders. Beyond the bridge, our land ended after about twenty feet and met the village path leading to the houses where the rest of our clan lived. At night, drunks staggered up the path on their way home. Some would slouch home quietly while others would shout in English. They made a comical picture.

Next to the bamboo grove was a wide yard where the younger children played, and close to the house was my own little flower garden. The house looked beautiful with the flowers blooming around it all year round. Wisteria climbed up the east wall. It looked pretty and Mother didn't mind it because it rarely attracted caterpillars. On the west wall, she had her purple grapes growing luxuriantly.

Father was the keener gardener of the two. His orchard lay beyond the house and spread in both directions. He loved to plant different fruit trees and experimented with varieties not usually found in these hills, so we had a scrawny apple tree that bore a single fruit once in two years and a coffee plant that gave very bitter fruit. Around them grew native plum, peach and guava trees.

Below the bathroom, which was really an outhouse, stood a jackfruit tree and the Doric plum that Father was so proud of. The upper garden had a low wooden fence running along one side, marking the boundary between our neighbour Jimmy's land and ours. Behind the kitchen, in the backyard, Mother planted seasonal vegetables like garlic, beans and mustard. To the west, where there was a shady spot in the backyard, grew several mint plants. But we didn't have much use for mint, except to put it in the occasional chutney.

On Saturdays, the Nepali women would come by, selling milk. 'Ama!' they would call out to Mother. Occasionally, they brought chicken or mustard leaves for sale. 'Ama, we have brought chickens today,' they would announce. Mother would invite them into the house and serve them tea. She said it wasn't right to send them away empty-handed.

'Ama, can we pluck some mint leaves?' one of the women sometimes asked. She was an especially large woman with very red cheeks, her name was Maya.

'Take what you want,' Mother would reply.

Maya would make her way to the back garden through the kitchen. She always took out the weeds around the mint bushes and plucked only as much mint as she needed.

The Nepalis lived in Aradura in tiny sheds in the forest. They bred cows and goats and chickens. Some of them also lived in the D-block colony. They had lived in Nagaland for a long time and were accepted as part of the community. The ones who lived at Aradura had built their huts deep in the woods so one couldn't see from afar that there was anyone living there.

We enjoyed the Saturday visits from the Nepali women. They wore colourful waist-cloths and told Mother how their cows were doing. All their cows had names: Maili, Saili and Priya. Once, one of the women, Maya's sister, was badly injured when she fell into the river while cutting grass. Mother and I went to see her in the hospital. Maya was there too, and she said, 'Oh, Ama, if there had been no one to bring her to the hospital, she would have died from the bleeding.' Maya's sister Sangeeta had a nasty cut on her forehead and lost a lot of blood. She had to be in hospital for a week. When her family visited, she asked after Priya and Maili and Saili. The doctor thought they were her sisters and was surprised to hear that Priya was refusing to give milk in Sangeeta's absence.

The hospital was in the middle of the town, an old building with few rooms. There were doctors there but no qualified nurses. Some Angami women worked as attendants. There were not many beds and no major surgeries were performed in Kohima. The hospital staff was gradually supplemented by Naga doctors who had finished their medical studies. Dr Neilhouzhü, the first Naga doctor, was already working in the hospital before the war.

In these pre-war years, there was a steady rhythm to our lives in our little town. Every morning we saw the same sights. On our way to school, we met the villagers of Kohima on their way to the fields. They carried their spades and daos in their baskets. Their terraced fields lay both east and west of the village. Every evening, as they returned home, we exchanged greetings.

But certain changes became quite visible at the beginning of 1942. For one, aeroplanes flew over our skies for the first time. This was such an amazing phenomenon for us that people talked about it for days. The men said that the aircraft that flew over our town were dakotas on their way to and from Imphal, where the British army had their airfield.

The dakotas were large, grey planes that flew low over Kohima. They created great excitement among the villagers and people would shout to each other whenever they heard the drone of an aeroplane. Many villagers feared them because they were so strange and new, but we in the town slowly got over our fear. Zhabu and Aneiü liked to run out and stand on a prominent open space as soon as they heard a plane approach. As it came overhead, they would wave their arms about and shout, 'Hey pilot, hey!' Sometimes the pilots waved back at them. That would be enough to make them feel thrilled all day.

In the middle of 1942, the British army began to enter our lands in larger numbers than we had ever seen before. There was a steady influx of army movement in our hills from then on. Army convoys became more frequent on the Dimapur–Kohima highway. The destination for some of the convoys was Kohima while others drove on to Imphal in Manipur. In the dry months, the convoys left the highway dust-choked as it had no asphalt work on it yet, and in summer the roads were quite muddy from the rain. It was not unusual to see trucks, with their wheels slipping in the mud, being pushed back onto the road by soldiers. When that happened, it slowed down the highway traffic considerably.

The new troops were made up of different nationalities. There were Pathans and Sikhs, along with some Negros, as we called them then. An equally large number of white soldiers, mainly British, were amongst the new troops. While some of them settled in the Assam Rifles camp area, the others spread out and set up camp at other places such as Garrison Hill, the hospital area, the Mission Compound and Peraciezie. The Mission Compound grounds were turned into a parking area for army vehicles. Before the end of the year, the preparations for war were very apparent. As for the civilian population, it seemed incongruous that the normal tenor of life would proceed in the midst of all these preparations for war. Yet, could anyone have lived differently?

The thing that alarmed us most was the occasional sound of distant gunfire at the end of 1942. From Kohima, we could distinctly hear it. The first time we heard it was late

one evening, when we were all at home. The next day when
we went to school, Reverend Supplee and our teachers said
they had received orders to teach us safety measures to
follow in the eventuality of a war. They led us to a corner
of the school compound where we all took turns at digging
trenches. Then we were told what we should do if we were
caught in the middle of a war and heard sirens. At the end
of the day, we went home in great excitement.

March 1943

In 1943, the war that had seemed such a distant thing for so long, finally reached us. It began with hordes of refugees that the Japanese invasion had pushed into our lands. They came in wretched bands; starving, diseased dregs of humanity, droves of them dropping down dead by the roadside or in the refugee camps. The Burmese refugees, as we called them, were not ethnically Burmese but largely of Tamilian stock, for many Tamilians had settled in Burma as traders before the war. They carried their belongings with them, in little boxes or bags, and many had bleeding feet as they had walked a very long distance barefoot.

They came straggling down the Imphal–Kohima highway, crossing the southern Angami villages. They had trekked through the torturous terrain of swamps and disease-ridden forests between Burma and the Naga Hills. A few of them begged the local people to give them refuge and the locals did so, taking them into their own households and sharing with them what they had. But no one really had very much to share. Those who reached Dimapur were placed in a camp where the British government provided them with food and shelter. That camp came to be known as Burma Camp.

For many Nagas, these were the first sights of what war could do to humanity. The war became a reality that sank in as more and more of our young men left home to join the army, the RAF and the navy. Uneducated men were recruited to work as coolies in Moreh and Tamu, carrying ammunition and supplies for the army. The army also paid labourers to work in Tiddim in Burma. Those who went to work in Tiddim were away for months. Even grown girls left home to join the military nursing service.

One afternoon, Rev Supplee called all the students together. We knew it was serious because he looked really sad. He said: 'My dear students, I have two big announcements to make today. Firstly, we have heard that the Japanese are preparing to invade India. Secondly, the school has been ordered to close down, because it is no longer safe for students and teachers. It will reopen after the war has ended. When that will be is difficult to predict now. I want all of you to pray for the war to be over soon. And I wish you all very well in your lives.'

We were shocked and saddened. It had never happened before that school was closed down.

What would we do? That was the big question everyone asked. The boys began to make their own plans. I overheard Jimmy and his friends saying, 'We could go to Tiddim, they won't ask how old we are.'

'Jimmy, don't do anything crazy!' I couldn't help telling him. 'Father says Tiddim is really far from here.'

'We wouldn't go without our parents' permission,' he said. 'Besides, it would be so wonderful. We could earn so much money!'

Jimmy and his siblings lived directly above our land. They often came to our house and we visited theirs. Jimmy was two years younger than I was, but being a boy, he would get up to all sorts of things. I envied his liberty. It was impossible for us girls to do anything adventurous, as our parents were very protective of us. Moreover, I was still underage so I could not join the nursing service, which was what I longed to do.

In the weeks that followed, more and more aeroplanes began to fly over our hills. Some of these, we were told, were reconnaissance aircraft, sent out to check on Japanese movement in the Burmese territories. In 1943, intermittent bombing began in the valleys east of Kohima. We were all terrified by it and felt fearful and uncertain. Rumours were rife that the Japanese had sent spies to Kohima and to the southern Angami villages.

Earlier in March, four Angami boys were arrested on the suspicion that they were Japanese spies. One of them was Jimmy's cousin. Rev Supplee was asked to identify them.

'These are all students of mine,' he said. 'I know them personally and can vouch that they are law-abiding citizens.' The boys were let off after that, but the incident added to the tension. We later discovered that it was indeed true that some Japanese had entered Viswema the year before. Impersonating Manipuri labourers, they worked on a school-building construction and took back elaborate maps of landmarks in the Imphal–Kohima area.

After the Mission School was closed down in 1943, the missionaries, Rev Supplee and his wife and children left for America. Their house was quickly turned into an army officers' residence for the division commandants. In the beginning, it felt very odd that school was closed, but there were so many other things happening that we soon got distracted.

There was the noise and bustle of great activity in those days. We grew used to the movement of troops by night and the building of new roads by the Kohima Garrison Engineers. Roads were being built along the Jessami track, on the Bokajan road towards Meriema, and the Indo–Burma road and the Imphal–Kohima–Dimapur highway were widened. The constant whirring of engines was a sound we would always associate with these days of suspense and fear.

I suppose there was a great deal of road building to be completed, for the Corps Royal Engineers were now issuing invitations to civilian contractors to build the new roads under their supervision. The Engineers were in a hurry to build these new roads. So there were a large number of young men and women from Kohima village who took up construction work.

While road-widening was the main work along the highway, the British Army Engineers were employing local Naga contractors to build new roads on the existing mud paths so that jeeps could ply on them. Some new roads were also being cut through the jungles, and bushes and trees had to be cleared to do this.

One afternoon, a young woman named Kasano and her brother came from the village to see me. I knew them fairly well as they were friends of Marina. They asked me to join them in a road contract. That would have been unheard of in peacetime. But there was a war now and the British administration was in a great hurry to build the roads.

'We have talked to Chaha. He says we need another member. They are desperate to get people to work on the roads. There is good money in it.'

'Which Chaha did you talk to?' I asked.

'Oh, it was the Cha Chaha,' Kasano said. 'There won't be any complications. But you know the Britishers always follow certain rules so he insists on four members.' Our people addressed all the British officers as Chaha. The road engineers were called Cha Chaha or 'boss of the road' to differentiate them from the other Chahas. Finally, I agreed to their request as there wasn't much to do with the school closed down.

The two of them met my father and asked, 'Apuo, will you allow Aviü to be a member of our contract group? We are three already and Chaha says he will give us the contract if we have a group of four. We have begun the work on the Bokajan road.' My father was a stern man and most of the younger people feared and respected him. He could be very caring too but people rarely saw this other side of him. I never really expected him to agree but he did, and so I joined the group of contractors.

Our work took us fourteen miles away from Kohima to the Bokajan road. The road construction work began below the village of Keruma. The hill was steep in many places, and the men were digging into the hillside itself. The new road would emerge very close to Dimapur town, crisscrossing northern Angami territory. The jungles around were thick and unaffected by the cold of winter. There we supervised the work of the labourers, mostly men from the Sema regions. They were good workers, and the road soon took shape. I did not have to stay at the site, but as a member of the team, I had to make occasional visits.

The road was dusty and always alive with the Royal Engineering officers driving up and down all day in their jeeps and bulldozers. After six weeks of supervising and translating, I was quite relieved to see it all come to an end. With spring around the corner, I welcomed the opportunity to stay at home and plant lily bulbs and tend to the orchids.

April 1943

4 APRIL

I wonder if I would ever have met Vic if I had said no to the next contract job. I'm just glad I said yes. When we were well into spring in the new year, Kasano paid me another visit. It was a sunny morning. Sam and I were running a little business at the time, selling ladies' garments and shoes which we ordered from *Hall and Anderson,* the army and navy store in Calcutta. Kasano bought a few things. Then she turned to me and asked, 'Aviü, can you join me and my brother in another contract work group?'

'No,' I said firmly, 'I found the first one quite tiresome. We had to travel such a distance every day.'

'It won't be like that this time,' she assured me. 'The work is closer to Kohima. It is on the Bokajan road. My brother and I, we have already got the contract. All we have to do is finance my brother and he will look after most of the work. Of course, we will have to go to the site sometimes but it won't be as strenuous as the last time.'

I was not very eager but she was persuasive. When I was

quite convinced that I would not need to go to the worksite as often as before, I agreed to join them.

After a few days, I accompanied Kasano to the worksite to find out how the work was getting on. The digging had gone well. But there was a lot of dust on the new roads as April was one of the driest months. In addition, there was a blue haze over the valley which made everything look like a dream. It was like the haze that came in February, a thin low-lying fog that covered the valleys throughout the month. It covered the green hills from early morning till late afternoon.

After some time, Kasano and I finished supervising the labourers and went into a shed to drink tea. It was just at that moment that two of the Royal Engineers came into the tea shed. They greeted Kasano and joined us. She introduced me to them. The taller of the two was a handsome young man called Staff Sergeant Victor. His friend Bob was stockily built and had very red hair. Sgt Victor kept staring at me. I felt awkward and tried to look away. But after a few minutes, he walked over and sat down beside me.

Taking both my hands in his, he said, 'You are the most beautiful girl I have ever seen. What's your name? Can you speak English?' I was overwhelmed by a variety of emotions – deep embarrassment, awe and fear at the unveiled admiration of this grown man.

I blushed and tried to turn away, but he clutched my hand tightly. 'Meet me tomorrow,' he pleaded. 'Let me take you out.'

When I remained quiet, he changed tactics. 'May I come to your house and meet your family? I could pick you up and take you out to tea,' he said. Still, I could not respond. For many reasons. We had barely met and my parents were very strict with us and particular about who we made friends with. And a strange white man calling on me at home? I did not think that would be a good idea at all. Oh, I knew Mother would be polite, she was never rude; but she would be polite in that inscrutable way of hers where you instinctively knew that she was sizing you up and it made you feel nervous and clumsy all at once.

I bowed my head and just shook my head at his repeated requests. 'Come here tomorrow then,' he urged. He must have noticed that I was extremely nervous because after some time, he turned his attention to the radio and played some music. Kasano and I got up to leave after we had drunk our tea. Sgt Victor came up to me when we were leaving and said, 'Please do come again, please.' I nodded ever so slightly and walked out of the shed hurriedly.

When I got home, Mother had made chicken for supper but I could barely eat.

'What's the matter? You're not coming down with a fever, are you?' asked Mother, noticing my lack of appetite.

'No, no,' I replied. 'I must have drunk too much tea,' I added lamely.

Mother stopped questioning me and we cleared away the pots and plates. We kept the fire burning because Mother and Father always drank tea after supper.

Afterwards, my sisters wanted to go for a walk, so I joined them. We didn't go very far. The hills in the distance were just black outlines. It soon got dark and all we could see were the lights slowly coming on in the houses. There were a few vehicles on the Kohima–Dimapur highway. We watched them until they disappeared from sight. Then the first stars came out and we headed back home.

I didn't sleep very much that night. I kept seeing Sgt

Victor's face in my mind and I thought about what he had said. Was this what falling in love was like? Was I falling in love?

That evening Kasano came by to deliver a message. Victor was asking to meet me at her house the next day.

5 APRIL

I was edgy all morning and waited impatiently for afternoon to come. Then, before Father came home from office, I got dressed and slipped out of the house. Mother was busy weaving and did not notice – or so I hoped.

Vic, as he had asked me to call him, was waiting for me at Kasano's place. He was as tall and handsome as ever and his face lit up with a smile as soon as he saw me. I think I fell in love with him then, or maybe I loved him the very first time I saw him. I begged Kasano to come with us and the three of us climbed into Vic's jeep.

Vic took us to see the Corps Royal Engineers camp and we sat in the room he shared with his friend Bob, and he played all the songs of Bing Crosby that I liked. We drank tea and ate biscuits. I was so shy that I could not respond to any of his questions. And he had so many of them! I tugged at Kasano's sleeve and bade her sit between the two of us because I felt so very nervous. 'Hou, Aviü!' she said in an exasperated voice. But she did consent to sit in the middle.

It was an odd conversation. Vic would ask me something and I would mumble my answer to Kasano and she would repeat it to Vic. He asked how old I was and a few questions about Father and Mother. Did I like him, he asked. I refused to answer. Kasano said something to him and he laughed.

Vic was very eager to find out how he could meet my parents and visit me with their permission. It made me worry that we would be forbidden to meet if he tried that. As we were talking thus, he suddenly leaned right across and smiled at me. It was so unexpected that I blushed and cried out in surprise and held up my hands to cover my face. They both laughed. But he moved away until I calmed down. We didn't stay very long after that. I was so embarrassed I begged to be taken home.

On our next meeting, I was a little more composed. Kasano came with me again. 'Cho! Aviü,' she said to me, 'he is a good man. Talk to him.' I managed a few sentences and Vic was very pleased. He drove us out of town towards Jakhama. The view from there was breathtaking – because we could see the entire village of Kohima and the villages beyond.

The skies in April are always so clear. From where we stood, we got a good view of the entire landscape. Stubbled rice fields were being ploughed in preparation for the year's cultivation. People were at work in their fields, burning the dead grass. Though the worst of winter was over, it was still quite chilly. When we had been standing and looking at the view for some time, a cold breeze blew up and I shivered.

'Oh, are you cold?' asked Vic. Before I could respond, he had draped his jacket over my shoulders. We drove back soon after that because the sun was going down.

A week went by before we could meet again. I was grateful for this in a way. It gave me some time to think about what was happening in my life now. I had so much on my mind. Did people fall in love in wartime? I asked myself. I never would have thought that was possible, but I missed Vic and looked forward to seeing him again. I even said little prayers for him at night.

In the middle of the week, Mother said we were going to gather firewood from our land on Bayavu Hill, an hour's walk away. We took some food and water with us. It was peaceful in the woods and we took our time, filling our baskets with the wood that workers had already cut and stacked on the boundary of our land.

'Is that too heavy for you?' asked Marina as she loaded my basket.

I tried lifting it. 'No, I can manage,' I reassured her as we helped each other with our loads.

Mother carried quite a lot of wood and the three of us walked homeward with our heads bent over from the weight. We always took a little jungle path home, so we rarely met anyone on our way back. I always enjoyed that; it was quiet and pretty with the flowers and bushes all around. I had plucked some pretty fern earlier and decorated my basket with it. If there had been more time, Marina and I would have gathered herbs.

Once we were on the highway, we took a short rest by the roadside. I looked up whenever an army jeep passed. But none was driven by Vic. The roads were not dusty as it had rained a while in the late afternoon. The new leaves on the trees held tiny raindrops that glittered in the sunlight. We didn't linger long though, because Mother wanted to get home early and start cooking for the evening meal.

The next day Kasano came by with a letter from Vic. She slipped it to me just as she was leaving.

'He's asked to meet you today,' she whispered.

'Oh, not today, couldn't I come tomorrow?' I pleaded.

'I'll tell him,' she said and left.

I didn't really have anything to do that day but I felt unready to meet Vic so soon. I hoped my emotions would settle a little by the time I saw him again. I read his letter at night when everyone was asleep. It was just a few lines long but I read them over and over. He had asked if we could meet and sent me all his love.

We met the following day. I felt nervous all over again at the sight of him. When we were alone, Vic said to me, 'I care for you very deeply, surely you can tell? I love you dearly.'

I couldn't respond. His words thrilled me and at the same time I was frightened by the intensity of his emotions. No one had ever said such things to me before. And I realized that I loved him back, this man who adored me and cared so much for me.

In the days we spent together, Vic was always patient with me, sensing my awkwardness and naïveté. Though he didn't look it, he was thirty when we met, devoted to his work and to me. Soon we were going out for picnics regularly with other friends of mine. My parents didn't object to us going out together as long as we were with a group of friends. And we found many excuses to go out – to gather herbs, pick wild flowers, or just for picnics and more picnics.

May–June 1943

Every day, or almost every day, we were together. Vic was extremely easy going. With older people, he was respectful and with younger ones, he could be playful. My friends would try to teach him words in Angami. This was a lesson that was always bound to end in great bales of laughter. Vic would struggle to say a sentence and it would come out all wrong. It was in these times that they all grew close to him.

'Vic said he would let me work in the camp,' Jimmy told me excitedly one day.

'Aren't you too young?' I asked anxiously.

'It's only to cut vegetables in the kitchen. Not other stuff,' he said and added that he would have his friends with him there.

Sometimes, Vic brought a ball along in the jeep and the boys would find some flat space to play with him. The boys enjoyed that very much. Some of them were eighteen and good players but they were never able to beat Vic. Jimmy would join them too, though he was even younger. They liked to play in the wide space in front of the Mission chapel, a little wooden house used by the missionaries to conduct services.

When we began to go out together, the rains were yet to set in so there were always lovely spots in the countryside for us to visit with our packed hampers. While we girls picked flowers after tea, Vic would remain sitting, watching us, smiling slightly. I suppose we must have seemed childish to him, running off suddenly as we did, to gather wild flowers or pick berries in season with great excitement.

Vic took us on long drives to the new roads, so that he could see how the road work was coming along. We drove past little Angami villages on our way. He would tell me, 'I want to show you off to all my friends and to everyone I know.' Though I was still quiet and didn't speak much with him, the others chattered away and Vic grew close to our circle of friends: Jimmy, Marlene and George and my sister Zhabu.

When we girls were on our own, we only talked about Vic. Marlene and Zhabu had so many questions.

'Aviü, what are you two going to do?' Marlene would ask. 'Will you marry him and go away to England? We'll never see you again.'

Then Zhabu would pipe up: 'Aviü, when you marry, you should stay here close to Mother and Father and the rest of us.'

There were many other things they wanted to know – what it was like to be in love, what he spoke to me about – especially because Vic was so much older than any of the boys we knew. At first, I told them we hadn't spoken about marriage yet. But we had. Vic had suddenly said one day that he wanted to marry me but I wouldn't let him speak any further. It was too early to talk of that.

Vic wrote me letters every single day. Kasano continued to bring them to me. On some days, he would bring the letter himself and ask me to read it later. His letters were full of affection for me, and he spoke of wanting the war to be over so that we could marry and live happily together. The days passed thus, with Vic spending as much time as possible with me and my friends. Even when he was away at work, he came to meet us in the evenings whenever he could. Then we would all go out in a big group, filling his jeep with songs and laughter.

At those times, we forgot about the war. It was wonderful to be young and in love, and in no fear of losing our near and dear ones. How young we were then. How thoughtless of what the future could bring. In later years, I would try to remember how we had spent those days. But I had no clear memories of them. Happy times leave no scars. The memories of loss are the ones that searingly remain.

October 1943

Everyone agreed that October was the prettiest time of the year, especially when the rains had retreated. Everything turned ripe yellow and it was a joy to see endless fields of golden paddy before the harvest. We spent day after day under gentle sunshine and clear skies. The hills turned gold, covered with the wild sunflower that bloomed in autumn and filled the landscape. It was the best month of the year.

The intense heat of the summer months had long left us and the bitter cold of winter had not yet set in. The frantic activity of the year had slowed down and before us lay long, balmy afternoons when the cicadas sang in the tall grass and the frogs took over from them in the evening. If it rained a little, nobody complained because the dry months were ahead of us and we welcomed a sudden shower, for it helped the vegetables and flowers to sprout and saved us a trip to the river.

One afternoon, Silie, one of our friends, invited us all to his orange orchard to pick fruit. 'If we don't pick them now, they'll fall off in the next week and they won't be good to eat any more,' he said. We didn't need a second invitation. When Vic came by, we clambered into his jeep and were off.

The orchard was beautiful. Some of the oranges were still green but most were ripe and the trees were bent heavy with fruit. All over the orchard, wild marigolds were blooming, fiercely blooming in an effort to overwhelm the spreading greyness on the ground, or so it seemed. We sat among the marigolds and had our picnic, savouring the roast chicken sandwiches that Vic had brought. He always made sure his men packed biscuits and chocolates for us, shipped all the way from England. It made Vic happy to see us eat well and he often brought gifts of food when he visited me at home.

After we had eaten, Silie and Marlene began to gather the ripe oranges into little baskets and Vic and I were left alone. I was suddenly very conscious of him sitting next to me. He took my hand and said, 'I love you, darling, I love you so dearly.'

I blushed deeply and didn't reply. I loved him just as much but was too shy to tell him so. It was as though I didn't have the words yet.

Vic turned to face me and said, 'I want to spend my life with you, will you marry me?'

I lowered my head and wondered what to say to him. I was so nervous my palms grew clammy and I pulled my hand away.

My heart beat rapidly. Marriage was such a big, big step. Of course I wanted to marry him, I was certain I loved him, but this was not the way marriages were contracted among our people. A young man's parents would send a paternal aunt to ask for the hand of the girl of his choice. But this, heavens, this was the sort of thing that happened in movies, the sort of thing I read about in books. And to think that it was happening to me now, at this very moment!

Vic went on. 'I must meet your parents. Say you love me, my dear one, say I love you Vic, more than anything in the world.'

Wild horses couldn't have dragged those words out of me. I remained sitting there, close to him, unable to utter a word.

I played with a bunch of marigolds in my lap and as I played with them, he said, 'Talk to me, dear one, tell me you love me too.' But I just sat there silently.

Suddenly he reached forward and took my hand in his. I was so nervous I balled my hand into a fist. The marigold petals I had been playing with were crushed between my fingers and their strong perfume suffused the still air.

Vic slowly pried my fingers open. He blew on my palm so that the bruised yellow petals fell to the ground. Still holding my hand, he said, 'Listen, I'll call you Marigold, my Mari, do you mind?'

I shook my head shyly.

Then he asked me to marry him again and said he would talk to my parents and finally, I found the courage to whisper yes.

After that day, Vic became a part of our family. All the children in our colony knew him. They would run after his jeep when he came to visit and he'd stop and let them clamber in as he drove up the steep road to our house. He would always come with gifts for me; I had never received so many gifts before.

My family found Vic easy to get along with. When he first came to our house, he explored the rooms eagerly, instead of sitting formally in the living room. He went down with

Father to look at his orchard and new fruit trees. By his second visit, he had made himself quite at home and sat in the kitchen while Mother cooked. He ate her cooking happily and endeared himself to her.

'He is a kind man,' said Mother observantly. Vic didn't mind Mother's smoke-filled kitchen at all: as a matter of fact, he was rather fond of it and thought it was homely.

Once Vic had been accepted into my family, I was a lot less shy with him. We talked more. On some evenings, we would sit together for a long time and he would tell me about his life in England and all the friends he had left behind. I was grateful that all my family members liked him. It made it so much easier for us to court. Of course, his work meant that he kept long hours and was away for several days at a time. But when he was free, he was always with us at our home.

December 1943

Christmas came around so quickly that year. I have always remembered Christmas 1943 as the best Christmas of my life. That morning, Father told us to hurry, so we were dressed and on our way to church when the bell tolled for the first time. The church was overcrowded and we knew we were lucky to have got seats right in front. The pastor preached on the birth of Christ and after the service there was a big feast.

The men had stayed up all night to slaughter two pigs and one cow and cook them in huge pots. This was served with rice and gravy on plantain leaves. Everyone had dressed well, the young men in new trousers and bright new body-cloths, the girls in new waist-cloths. A few of the girls wore dresses and new shoes. The girls senior to us at school wore the flared skirts that had been the rage all summer. I wore a new dress that Vic had bought me. It had a wide flared skirt and I wore a little red coat with it.

Afterwards, Vic, Lt Morris and Bob came home to greet us. We played our favourite songs on the gramophone Vic had given me. Over and over, Bing Crosby sang 'White

Christmas', 'Silent Night', 'Blue Hawaii' and 'Road to
Morocco'. My youngest sister Aneiü and two cousins her
age danced to the songs. How happy we were that day.

On New Year's Eve, our neighbours, the 253 Sub-area Signal
Boys, had a big campfire in front of their mess. They invited
all the young men and women from our neighbourhood to
join them. We felt very grown-up as we went in a big group
to celebrate the new year with the soldiers.

Marlene and I wore long skirts and high heels. She had a
pink lipstick with her, which we both put on before leaving
the house. Jimmy had on his brandy-coat and woollen
trousers. The Signal Boys served us tea and cakes baked by
their cooks. Later in the night, plates of chicken sandwiches
appeared. We began by playing some games, but later
people sat around the fire and just sang song after song all
night long.

We sang 'Daisy Daisy', 'You are my Sunshine' and
'Kohima will Shine Tonight' with gusto. Supplee's song on
Kohima, written before the war, was quite popular amongst
the soldiers:

Kohima will shine tonight,
Kohima will shine.
When the sun goes down
and the moon comes up,
Kohima will shine.
K-O Ko, H-I Hi, M-A Ma spells Kohima.
There's no place in this world
half as fair as Kohima.

We sang in unison, over and over again. Towards morning,
people's voices sounded tired but none of the night's gaiety
was lost. How joyful we were, it was difficult to believe we

were in the middle of a war. Our parents readily allowed us to enjoy these days with our friends. Perhaps they knew that it would be a long time before we could celebrate anything again.

The best part about Christmas was that Vic was able to spend the whole week with us. The men made up teams, one with the Mission Compound boys and the other with the Signal boys and they played three football matches on New Year's Day. Both teams played so fiercely that the first two matches ended in a tie. It had grown dark by then but they rigged up lights so that the third match could be played. The matches continued over the next two days, joined by a team of boys from the town.

In the following weeks, Kohima returned to normal. The festivities were over and we tried our best to get back into the rhythm of daily life. It was a little difficult. But our daily chores around the house quickly restored the rhythm of day-to-day life.

February 1944

Soon after the new year, Mother sowed new seeds in her vegetable garden. I, too, planted some flower seeds in the front yard. I replanted the dahlia and lily bulbs in a shady spot. The rose bushes would be all right in the sun. The soil was still hard but if we had a few showers the flowers would bloom. Relatives from the village came visiting before they got too busy with work on their fields.

The school remained closed but students found other things to do. I thought our school building was beginning to look dilapidated because it had been unused for so long. On the east wall, the broken windowpanes had not been replaced.

Some of the older boys from our school left for Tiddim to work as labourers. Jimmy went with them. After two months, he came home for good. Everyone gathered round him in the evening and listened to stories about the preparations for war in Tiddim. Jimmy and his friends had worked on road-digging in the area. They were paid well. Jimmy said some of the local people at Tiddim could speak English. He had also learnt a few Burmese words.

He said there were many more warplanes flying back and forth.

It was one of the reminders that a war was close at hand. We saw other signs around us. Kohima had become very different from the peaceful little hamlet we had grown up in. There was movement all around. Every day, you could see more and more British, Indian and Gurkha troops coming into Kohima and camping all over the place. There were soldiers everywhere. The preparations for war that had been suspended for the Christmas celebrations seemed to have resumed with renewed energy.

The winter months were dry months in our land. The military jeeps and vehicles left a trail of dust wherever they went and Kohima began to look like it was covered by a constant grey fog.

The new roads to the north of Kohima were not tarmacked. When the dust settled, one could see long brown tracks snaking their way down towards Dimapur. Some more roads were still being built in the new year.

There were many new soldiers – we knew this for we were well acquainted with the ones who had been here for the past two years. On Sunday evenings, the Mission chapel was packed with British troops and officers, many coming from far-off camps for the service in English. They walked into the small church with their loaded rifles on their shoulders. At such times, we felt sobered by the reality of the war that was drawing closer to our lands every day.

Vic often took me to the service. Many times, we felt the abiding presence of God in the gathering gloom, the helplessness of a life overwhelmed by death, where a person's faith in God was the only sure thing he could rest upon. Vic was very quiet and deep in thought whenever he came visiting now.

One day in late January, Vic asked me to go with him to the new border road to Jessami, where some of his contractors were working. On our way back home, four of his contractors joined us and they sat in the rear seat of the one-ton truck. Vic was left-handed but he could drive well with his right hand.

The roads were narrow and treacherous in parts, because there were sharp turns on the road every half a mile. We were about six miles from Kohima when the whole world seemed to cave in on us. One moment we were laughing at a joke someone had cracked, and the next moment there was a great crashing sound and I felt myself flying through the air. The truck had overturned at one of the sharp bends in the road and I was thrown out.

I was cut badly on my forehead and my face was full of blood. I must have lost consciousness. When I slowly came to, I heard voices from far away, Vic picking me up and crying, 'Oh, God, please, don't take her away, I love her more than anything in the world.'

I fainted again.

All I remember is hearing Vic's voice as though from a great distance. Over and over I heard him praying, 'Please, God, don't let her die.'

Afterwards, they told me that a three-ton truck carrying troops of the Assam Regiment came along. The driver quickly unloaded the soldiers he was carrying and took us to the hospital in Kohima. One of Vic's friends had a fractured arm and the others escaped with a few bruises and cuts. Vic had managed to hold onto the steering wheel and avoided being flung out.

At the hospital, they cleaned the wounds on my forehead. I had bled profusely, giving Vic the impression that I was possibly dead. I was bruised all over and felt as though I had broken a few ribs. When I regained full consciousness, I hurt everywhere.

Mother and Father came as soon as they heard. My younger sisters were in tears when they saw my wounds. The doctor comforted them and reassured them that he would give me some medicines to make me all right again. He told them he had to keep me in the hospital to make me better. That calmed them down.

They must have sedated me on the first night because I slept for almost two days. The hospital staff was very kind to me. Every morning, the nurse came to clean my wound. Then she changed the dressing. I felt so dizzy I collapsed whenever I tried to stand on my feet. I thought I had probably broken something. In the following days, I tried to move around my room, taking a few weak steps at a time. In spite of my fears, I had not broken any bones. But I had been so badly thrown that I had great difficulty moving.

I had to stay in hospital for a month. Vic came to see me every day, bringing flowers and presents. He was just so grateful we had been given another chance. The accident made us realize just how fragile life was, that we had no control over it, and being given another lease on it was a precious gift.

Finally, I was back at home but I was still very weak. Vic returned from a ten-day trip to Calcutta for his promotion exams, bringing back jewellery, dresses, shoes and a watch for my birthday. But I was happiest with the platinum ring that he had brought for our engagement.

On Sunday Vic came by very early to spend the day

with my family. He sat with Father for a long time. I served them tea but did not stay in the room. They were deeply engrossed in a discussion about our future and it made me very nervous. Father had agreed to our marriage and we were engaged that evening. I hoped to be better by February or March so we decided that the wedding would take place then. We were both happy with this arrangement and I made sure I rested for long periods so I would regain my strength faster.

March 1944

It was wonderful to be engaged to Victor and he was the most caring person I knew. We couldn't wait to get married. But when March came, the situation was very different. News arrived that the Japanese were just days away from Kohima.

Since Father was a treasury officer in the district commissioner's office, he had to leave quickly for Shillong, carrying important documents and money. Most of the officers of the British army were ordered to Dimapur.

Vic came to live with us, moving all his belongings into our house. That would have been unacceptable in peacetime. But everyone seemed to realize that we were living in unusual times and Vic and I were treated as though we were as good as married. We were grateful for that and we spent as much time together as we could manage, though Vic had to be away at the camp for long hours. He still supervised the remaining road work. In our culture, Vic coming to live with me made us a married pair. But we both wanted a church wedding after the war.

By the end of March, Kohima was like a ghost town.

A wedding was out of the question now. The traders at Kohima, who were mostly plainsmen, had fled to Dimapur and beyond, having sold their shops or closed down their shutters when they could not sell. Long gone were the open markets and hawkers that added so much colour to the town. The Manipuri women, with their wares of dried fish and peanut brittle and jaggery, were missing. The local people escaped to the Angami villages in the north, to Tsiesema, Rükhroma and other northern villages where they could live in relative safety. The army had its own supplies and the rest of us who had not left learned to do without certain food items.

With the shops closed, there was no movement on the streets. No one loitered around any more and the vegetable market looked run-down, bereft as it was of shopkeepers and buyers. At first, some of the traders sold goods from their homes. But that stopped in two or three days. The town was no longer safe for civilians.

Every half hour, the army jeeps would drive past in a tearing hurry. Apart from that, there was no sign of life in Kohima. There were some stray dogs on the streets. That was all. The few who remained behind were in the process of either leaving or packing to leave Kohima.

Vic was very worried for our safety. With Father away in Shillong, he took charge of our family. On 30 March 1944, he took my younger sisters to Chieswema, seven miles from Kohima. They stayed there with an uncle of ours. Zhabu and Aneiü had been taken to Chieswema twice before when word arrived that the Japanese had entered the eastern part of our lands. But after things quietened down, they were brought back to Kohima. So they didn't think it would be any different this time. It was a bit of an adventure for them, to be in the midst of a war and be evacuated back and forth.

By this time, all of Vic's friends knew about our engagement and they often exchanged duty with him so that he could be with me more. Now, when he came to stay for the night, he was fully armed, his loaded rifle on his shoulder and a row of shiny rifle shots on the strap. His kit bag was weighed down with grenades. When I saw the rifle for the first time, I couldn't sleep, but Vic would fall sound asleep with his rifle on one side and me on the other. He was mentally and physically exhausted and collapsed as soon as his head touched the pillow, falling into a deep, fatigued sleep. Most of the time he slept peacefully. Before dawn, he would be up and off to relieve his mates.

Many nights he told me, 'Marigold, we have to part for a few days, but not for long, I promise. I'll never leave you. No matter where I go, I'll come back to you. I want to stay here and defend your country and your people. Should the order come for me and my friends to move away from Kohima, I'll have to go wherever they send me. But I promise you I'll come back to you.'

It dawned on me then that the war was a very real thing and, seeing the seriousness on Vic's face and how heavily armed he always was when he came home, I knew that it was only a matter of days before our lives would be overwhelmed by it.

Perhaps he understood how frightened I was, or maybe he was trying to comfort himself, but Vic seemed to repeat the same words when we were together. 'We'll be parted for some days but not for long,' he would say each time.

Vic had good reason to worry because the sound of faraway gunfire had come much closer to Kohima. At night, we saw many flares go off in the distance. Whenever the sirens went off, we ran to the trenches outside and crouched until the sound of gunfire receded.

April 1944

3 APRIL

On the night of second April, Vic did not show up. I didn't worry at first. But it became increasingly lonely in the house with just Mother for company. My two sisters were away and I missed their laughter and teasing. They had been taken to my uncle's house in Chieswema. Sam felt they would be safer there and, when the need arose, the rest of us could join them. Chieswema was not on the main highway, so people thought it was safer from the Japanese.

Earlier that evening, when the sun was setting and the house filled with an orange glow, for a moment we seemed far removed from the terrible war raging around us. In the west, the sky was dark orange, almost scarlet, and for a while there was no sound of gunfire. The hills were outlined beautifully against the glowing sky. I stood outside and thought of my sisters and the happy life we had had in this house with our parents.

That happy life seemed to have passed in a flash and now everything was being threatened by war. There were so many rumours about the Japanese. Some of the men said the Japanese were short and ugly and some said they were like us and would treat us well. But there were many different reports and it was difficult to know what to believe. I hoped we would not fall into Japanese hands and be dealt with cruelly. The picture of the refugees who were fleeing the Japanese advance flashed in my head. Some of them bore marks of Japanese torture. There were young children in the group whose parents had been killed by the Japanese. I prayed we would not suffer that.

That night, everyone went to bed after dinner but I lay awake, thinking of Vic. I missed him sorely on the nights when he could not come home to me. When would the war be over so we could live a normal life together, I wondered. I did not feel sleepy at all. I lay awake, listening to sounds from outside or within. But it was always very quiet in our big house at night. My brother and his wife lived on the other side of the compound. I knew they and my mother were all fast asleep. Vic had failed to come and I was anxious and afraid. Suddenly, I heard the sirens wail. I jumped out of bed and ran to wake Mother but she was already up and pulling on her sweater. Sam and Bano ran over and we all headed for the trenches.

These trenches had been built in 1942 when the Japanese suddenly bombed Burma. They had been dug behind our house and were hidden behind a stone wall. We crouched in the trenches and braced ourselves. The sirens were swiftly followed by the bursting of grenades and the roar of big guns. We lay in the trenches, trying not to move. We lay there until the worst seemed to be over.

I feared for Vic, where was he? Was he in the midst of those bursting shells? When the firing died down, we returned to the house and the others went back to sleep but I remained awake, sitting in the downstairs room. I sat there for a long time, half praying and half crying for Vic to be safe. I tried to be as quiet as possible because I didn't want to wake Mother. Then I heard my name being called and the sound of frantic knocking.

'Aviü, open the door, please open the door!' It was Jimmy and his younger brother. I let them in. 'Did you hear the shots? They're coming closer and closer, we are so frightened!'

My brother and his wife woke and joined us and we all sat in the living room, huddled together, listening to the sounds of battle. My mother came after a while and spoke gently to us, 'Don't be afraid, God will not allow anyone to harm us. Just pray to God and ask for His protection.' After some time, she went back to her room.

The two boys went back to their house but after an hour, when we heard the sirens blaring once again, they came running back, calling out to me. I let them into our house.

Though nobody said it out loud, we knew we would not sleep again that night. We had never heard the sound of such intense gunfire before. And though we were well-drilled in what to do if the sirens sounded, it was terrifying to actually put it to practice. Over the past few weeks, we had grown used to hearing gunshots in the distance or the shelling of towns at a great distance from Kohima. Now, it seemed that those sounds had come closer, magnified and multiplied a hundred times.

The boys said their parents had forbidden them to leave the house till they returned from Zubza the next morning. But they were too frightened to stay on their own. Their house stood higher up on the slope than ours, so it was less sheltered from the gunfire.

Towards dawn, the noises died down at last. The silence that followed was eerie. The long night had made us accustomed to the intermittent sound of rifle shots and exploding grenades, and with each gunshot we prepared ourselves for more. Finally, when the noises had completely subsided, we went outside.

It was a strange sight. There were no jeeps or trucks in sight. The busy sub-area of Mission Compound, which used to be a hub of furious activity at all times, seemed to have dissolved in a single night. Not a soul was around.

While we stood there, watching this new, unfamiliar Kohima, Vic's jeep tore up the road and stopped in front of us. He jumped out and rushed up to me.

'Marigold!' he said breathlessly. 'Get ready quickly, there's no time. I'm taking you and the whole family to Chieswema where you will be safe. You have to stay there for a few days until this madness is over.'

I was too startled to reply.

'Don't worry,' Vic continued, 'I'll come and see you when I can. Now, come on, you have to get ready.'

I felt numb. I had not been prepared for this parting from Vic. Nor had the seriousness of the war fully dawned on me until the frightening experience of the night before. Tears blinded me and none of what Vic was saying made sense. I was not afraid of the enemy or of gunfire. But I couldn't bear the thought of separation from Vic in the midst of such uncertainty. If we were destined to die, I wanted to die by his side.

Gently leading me into the house, Vic began to pack a suitcase for me. He stuffed it with tinned food to last us a few weeks, some of my clothes and toiletries, whatever he felt I might need while away from Kohima. I kept wandering about the house aimlessly. The shock of having to leave Kohima was slowly sinking in.

Thoughts crowded my mind. What if I refused to leave? Would that put Vic in danger if he had to drive out to see me every night? From the west window I could see Garrison Hill and Aradura. Some trees and houses had been shelled in the night. The barricades on the road were clearly visible.

The town was so still, so ghostly in its quietness. No soldiers or vehicles or people around. The silence of that morning was like nothing I had ever known. How long would we have to be away? I had never lived through a war before and had no idea how long it would take before we could return home. And it occurred to me that we were going away from home indefinitely. I began to weep silently and forced myself to wipe my tears away. I looked around my home, trying to remember everything in it.

While Vic was still packing, we heard the sound of aircraft. Sam and I went to the back of the house to get a better look. There were three aeroplanes but they were flying too high for us to see which side they belonged to. But the whine of aircraft directly above our heads brought home the truth that Kohima was too exposed to shelling from either side.

'Vic is right,' said Sam, 'the sooner we leave, the better.'

I went back into the house for a last look at the packing. Vic's jeep was stuffed with our bedding and clothes. Bano had made neat bundles of food which she placed carefully in one corner of the jeep. Within an hour we were all ready to leave.

But Mother refused to go with us. No amount of persuasion would make her change her mind.

'I cannot leave my parents behind,' she said to Vic. To me,

she said, 'Don't worry about me, God will take care of me. Aviü, you must go and see to the younger ones.' Mother's aged parents were sheltering at Kitsubozou, the colony below Mission Compound. They had stubbornly refused to ever leave Kohima and Mother was determined to stay and look after them. Vic spent a long time persuading Mother to come with us but she would not leave.

Finally, the five of us – my brother, his wife and me and a woman called Vikieü and her baby – got into the jeep and Vic drove toward Chieswema. It was the third of April when we left Kohima. We knew it would be a long time before any of us would return.

The village of Chieswema was on top of a hill, as most Angami villages are. From the highway, there was a narrow path leading uphill to the village. Vic parked his jeep on the newly-built Bokajan road just off the highway and we walked up the path with our baggage. The path was steep and we climbed slowly.

As we were walking towards the village, Vikieü kept looking at Vic again and again, rather anxiously. She then turned to me and said, 'Aviü, tell Vic to take good care. Warn him not to drive so fast. I can see sudden death on his forehead. I can't tell you how or when, but I can see it very clearly.'

Her words made me worry even more. Vic always drove too fast. Even after the accident he would still drive very fast sometimes. I asked him to drive carefully. I don't think it entered anyone's head then that Kohima would be a battlefield where so many British, Indian and Gurkha forces would fall. We had such faith in the British government that we didn't believe it could be defeated by any other nation.

The British had always protected us and our land. I did not think that Vic could be in any great danger because of the war, but his rash driving worried me. Vic stayed with us all morning, helping us settle in and unpack our things.

At Chieswema, I was reunited with my younger sisters and there was some joy in that. They were missing Mother terribly but after we told them about the terrible shelling of the night before, they accepted that it was impossible to go back home now.

In the afternoon, Vic went back to his post on Garrison Hill. Before he left, he took out a photograph of me which he always carried in his wallet, with a bit of my hair tied in a ribbon. He said, 'Wherever I am, you are right next to my heart,' and he pointed to his heart. 'I love you, Mari. I am coming back to take you away when all this is over. Pray that the situation be over soon so we can be together. If the war takes longer, be brave and wait for me, darling. You mustn't let anything happen to you. If I'm away for long, wait for me. It would break my heart if you married someone else... You know I love you and want to look after you.' He held me gently and stroked my hair as he said this. 'Be safe, my dearest. Keep praying to God. Remember, I pray every night for you. I'll come tomorrow and see you and the family. As soon as I am free, I'll come to you.'

He hurriedly got into the jeep and drove off, waving at us. I stood and watched the jeep till it disappeared into the distance and all I could see was the trail of dust it left behind. We were safe now, Vic had seen to that, but I felt an emptiness inside me and wished I could shake it off. He had promised to return tomorrow, so why was this ache inside me refusing to die? I turned and went back into the house and busied myself with the rest of the unpacking.

But Vikieü stopped me. 'Don't unpack everything yet. We can't tell how long we can stay here. It might come suddenly,' she warned.

So I left the suitcase that Vic had packed for me untouched. Then I went to join the others at supper, which my aunt had cooked for us. She served us hot rice and meat. Sensing that we were missing Mother, she comforted us and said that we would not be parted for long. Her daughter was about Aneiü's age and they had become playmates.

4 APRIL

In the early afternoon of the fourth of April, we went down to the main road and waited for Vic. We waited until late but there was no sign of him or his jeep. From where we stood, we could see the vehicles moving along the Kohima–Dimapur road. But once it began to get dark, we gave up hope of him coming that day and returned to the village.

When we reached the wooden gate of the village, we heard the loud roar of guns and the sound of grenades and bombs exploding. We looked towards Kohima anxiously. The village faced Kohima directly and from where we stood, we could see the town and the houses on top of the hills. How shocked we were to see the whole of Kohima ablaze and covered with thick black smoke.

We could not believe our eyes. The peaceful and charming little town that had been our home all these years was going up in smoke! We stood there, transfixed; Zhabu held my hand tightly while Aneiü began to sob.

'This was why Vic couldn't come today,' said Vikieü in a low voice. I nodded but couldn't bring myself to speak.

My mind was a jumble of thoughts. How was Mother?

How was Vic? Were they alive? The thought that they might have been killed was too much to bear. We stood there for a long time.

It was dark when we made our way back to the house, choked with emotion and dazed from the sight of our beloved home burning and enveloped in black smoke. We could not speak to each other, so wrapped up in our own thoughts were we.

We were not the only ones who were anxious. By night, the council of elders in the village was conferencing over what was to be done next. Chieswema was only nine miles from Kohima, it would be just a matter of a few hours before the enemy was upon us.

Seeing Kohima burn was a great shock to all and showed everyone how vulnerable the British forces were. Now the villagers of Chieswema were trying to decide where they could go to seek refuge. It was paradoxical that a village that had offered refuge to others should now be worrying about seeking refuge itself.

That night, many Indian soldiers of the Assam Regiment came to Chieswema for shelter. They were soldiers who had escaped from Jessami and Kharasom in Manipur. The villagers supplied them with food and provided guides to lead them to the next village, Keruma, so they could join their unit at Dimapur.

5 APRIL

The village was a flurry of activity. Quite early in the morning people had begun to kill their cattle. We bought some meat from them and cooked it. While the five of us were staying with my uncle, Sam and Bano had gone to

stay with Bano's relatives in the neighbouring compound.
My brother and his in-laws were being given Naga haircuts
when we went across to their house.

The barber had cropped Sam's hair with a dao. He
chopped the men's hair straight across the back and sides,
so they would look like the other men of the village. Sam
and the young men who had been to school wore their hair
in the western fashion, making them an easy target for the
Japanese, who could pick them out and force them to work
as spies.

I went back to my uncle's house to help my aunt prepare
the morning meal. My uncle was still at Sam's house,
watching them get their haircuts and assisting the barber.

One man was posted at the top of the village to warn
the community if the Japanese approached. It was about
nine in the morning when he suddenly shouted, 'Many
soldiers coming this way, but they are not wearing British
uniforms and helmets. They are marching straight towards
our village!'

We were alerted in an instant. As my sisters and I ran
out to the square to get more news, we met Sam with his
new haircut. He was dressed in an old, torn shirt. Instead
of trousers, he wore the black kilt that the other men in
the village wore. All his in-laws were dressed in the same
manner. Sam was unusually fair, so he had rubbed ash and
charcoal on his neck where his fair skin was exposed.

The other men were dark-skinned, so they didn't need
the ash and water mixture to be smeared over them. The
Japanese were said to be so clever that they could pick out
the educated Nagas from among the villagers. They were
aware that the agricultural workers in the villages had little
knowledge of the area beyond their village territory. The

educated Nagas were more valuable to the Japanese, so disguising oneself became a matter of life and death.

Sam was taller than the other men. The villagers told him to avoid standing up and drawing attention to himself, so he mingled with them as best as he could and waited for the approach of the Japanese. Everyone seemed too petrified to even try to run away. The guard warned us again that the soldiers were approaching the village very fast. 'They're coming up like ants, and there are so many of them,' he shouted. The man cutting Sam's brother-in-law's hair was only halfway through his job when this second shout came. Hurriedly finishing the job, he was also made to blend in with the menfolk of the village.

The rest of us had changed out of our dresses and we wore faded woven Angami waist-cloths given to us by our relatives in the village. A woman came up and smeared ash and charcoal on my face, saying, 'My dear, I have to disguise your fairness or else the Japanese will know that you are not a village-dweller.' I looked around and saw that two other women were doing the same to my younger sisters. The coal stung my flesh but I gritted my teeth and waited for her to finish.

The sunburnt village women were prominently darker than the three of us. Sitting among the village women, we noticed that our arms and legs were also fairer than theirs, so we rubbed coal and ash all over our bodies and tried to sit unobtrusively amongst them.

When the Japanese marched into the village, people stopped what they were doing and stood still. We dared not stare at them openly but we managed to catch a glimpse of these men whom we had heard so much about. How we feared them. They were stockily built and looked very much like our men in many ways. Most of them had beards and their clothes were dirty and torn in places. They looked tired and hard-faced. I felt that these were men capable of anything. How terrifying they looked with their long bayonets pointing at us.

As the villagers shuffled back and stood in little groups, we were separated from my brother's family. Jimmy was with us, his hair half-cropped. He had been separated from his parents. We didn't want to draw attention to ourselves by seeking out Sam and Bano, so we huddled quietly with the rest.

We sat in the village square and watched as the Japanese entered my uncle's house and took our belongings. First, they took our clothes out of the house, our nice dresses and coats, and then they began to take our carefully stored rations. Tears stung my eyes when I saw the soldiers take away the coat Vic had given me. But I was helpless, I dared not protest. I fought back my tears and tried to sit very still. They took away Jimmy's brandy-coat, which he had been given when he went to work at Tiddim. Vic had stocked several tins of food for us when he brought us here. But now they fell into Japanese hands. The soldiers laughed and talked loudly to one another as they stuffed the clothes and food into their backpacks. My sisters and I sat with the villagers, looking at one another, tears glistening in our eyes.

The village of Chieswema was, by now, full of Japanese soldiers. They quickly set up their wireless systems. Some of them went up to the village people and demanded – in broken English – eggs, chickens, water and rice. One of them waved and signalled to Jimmy to get up. Jimmy stood up and went closer to him.

The soldier ordered him to go into the house and fetch eggs. Jimmy smiled and made gestures with his hands to show that there were no eggs. The soldier pushed an earthen jar into Jimmy's hands and told him to fetch water. Jimmy took the jar, but in the next moment he pretended to lose his grip on it. The jar fell to the ground and was smashed. The soldier muttered something angrily and slapped him hard.

Jimmy froze and turned red in the face as he struggled to stay calm. To retaliate would only end in a bullet. Everyone could see that. These first encounters with the Japanese were unpleasant, and it only grew worse. We feared their ruthlessness and were wary of drawing attention to ourselves.

It became apparent that the Japanese were going to stay on in the village. So the villagers prepared to leave. That evening my uncle told us, 'It will be better if you are taken to the woods. The Japanese presence will surely attract British bombing and it won't be safe for anyone. Your aunt will take you to a shed for the night.'

We got ready to leave the village. My aunt and her daughter led the six of us away: Jimmy, my two sisters and I, and Vikieü with her baby. We could not enter our house in the village because it was being guarded by soldiers. Besides, there was nothing left since they had taken everything of value. So we took some cooked food and left with my aunt. I was a little surprised we were not stopped but the Japanese did not seem to care whether we stayed or not.

We set out for the forest and walked on till we reached the Tsiekhou woods and found a cow-shed. These woods were mostly dense forest. The little cow-shed became our next home and we tried to make ourselves as comfortable as we could with the old woven cloths we had been given.

But it was April and winter not quite over; we felt very cold at night and missed the comforts we had taken for granted at home: warm beds and clean bedclothes, food that was well-cooked and always there for every meal.

At least we were safe for some time, at least we were away from the dreaded Japanese. This thought gave some comfort though we still worried for our parents and Vic. We missed Father too, but were reassured that he was safe in Shillong.

6 APRIL

My aunt and her daughter stayed with us in the night. When morning came, there was no food left. Mother and daughter left for the village, promising to send us food. Once they had gone, I felt desolate because I was responsible for my younger sisters and had no idea what to do. Vikieü could not be expected to help much because of her baby.

'What shall we do now?' I asked Vikieü rather desperately.

'We will have to wait, we mustn't go back to the village,' she said.

We spent all day in the shed. In the afternoon, we heard someone approaching.

'It's Neizielhou!' Aneiü cried out joyfully.

'I've brought a little rice,' said our cousin when we let him in. He had also brought my suitcase which held some of our rations. My uncle had, very thoughtfully, hidden the suitcase before the Japanese arrived. It contained all the things that Vic had packed, the clothes and toiletries. I was very grateful to get these back.

To our surprise, Neizielhou also brought the half of

Father's gun that we had carried from Kohima. We had brought it along to Chieswema for safekeeping. Neizielhou said, 'There are just too many Japanese soldiers back in the village. You had better take this with you. It's too dangerous for you to return. Stay here at Tsiekhou, I promise I will return tomorrow.'

When it was evening, we got ready to spend the night in the shed again. But as the light grew dim, we heard soft footfalls. Our hearts pounding, we waited and tried to be as quiet as possible. Could it be the Japanese come to capture us? Then to our great relief, we heard Sam's voice, 'Aviü, Zhabu, are you there?'

He had come with our cousin Siekuo. 'We walked all the way from Rükhroma village,' they said, explaining that they had used the wood paths for fear of being discovered by the enemy. How glad we were for their company. We shared the little food that we had and they stayed the night with us. After eating, we gathered straw and jungle leaves together to make mattresses for our makeshift beds.

As we were preparing to go to sleep, we heard the sound of a tiger growling outside. It was a terrifying sound, a low, angry rumbling. The men brought more firewood and fed the fire in an effort to keep the beast away. It was a moonless night and we couldn't see the animal but we could all hear its growling at short intervals.

Siekuo, the eldest among the men, said, 'Go to sleep, it will not harm us, we have done it no harm. Go to sleep, all of you, I'll keep watch.' He asked my brother to sleep too, while he kept watch, constantly stoking the fire.

My sisters slept but I lay awake, pretending to be asleep. After some time, my brother woke and relieved Siekuo. I heard snatches of their conversation. When the tiger growled loudly, Siekuo would ask, 'Samuel, what shall we do?' Sam would tell him we would be safe if we kept the fire going. The three of them took turns at keeping watch over us that night. When the tiger growled louder, they made loud noises too. We could smell the tiger's presence all night. Tigers have a distinct smell about them. It is a peculiar smell, like burnt feathers. It came in whiffs, stronger at some moments and faint at others, probably depending on his circling movements around the shed.

Morning came but it had been a restless night for us, with the sounds of shellfire in the distance and the fright from the tiger. The three men had to leave in the morning and rejoin their families. Sam had left his pregnant wife in the village of Rukhroma. They urged us to leave Tsiekhou. Zhabu too agreed that we should leave at once.

'Yesterday when Aneiü and I went to the stream to wash ourselves and gather herbs, I smelt the stench of a tiger,' Zhabu told us. 'I asked Aneiü if she could smell it. But she couldn't. I am sure the tiger had been prowling around us. Let's not linger here.'

At Sam's urging, we packed and moved to Chüzie. We all left together and after some time, Sam and Siekuo took the road to Rükhroma. Sam would travel further from there to Kohima to report for duty as a King's Scout and Siekuo would rejoin his family. They promised to return as soon as they were able to.

It was just as well that we left because Tsiekhou was a very isolated place with no other people around. Chüzie was an encampment where many of our village people now lived.

After hours of walking, we came to a field with a thatched hut where we found a woman with her three children. She was from Kohima village. She said we could share the hut with them. She looked like she was in her forties but her children were all quite young.

The woman told us that the Japanese had taken her husband away and she was not sure if they would release him. However, she told us that Biaku was only a mile or two away and many from Kohima village were camped there.

'What shall we do?' we asked one another. Finally, we decided we would press on towards Biaku but not right away: we would stay here till morning. Borrowing a hoe from the woman, we dug a trench in one corner of the field – this was what we had been taught to do wherever we camped.

Though we were relieved to hear that Biaku was not far away, we were worried about what the woman told us about it. 'Biaku is very crowded,' she said, 'and the Japanese often come and take away the men. In addition, they take the food the people have scavenged for themselves.' In this way, the Japanese alienated the local population completely by taking away what little food they had. The other danger in these woods was that the overwhelming presence of the Japanese attracted fire from British bombers.

We stayed at the hut for a few more days, trying to decide what to do.

8 APRIL

It was perhaps the worst month to be camping outside. In the dry months of March and April, up until early May, very few edible herbs are to be found in the woods. We gathered some gajo and gazie. That was about it. There are no fruits in this season either, no fish in the dry or partially dry streams. We were hungry and lonely. The cold at night added to our woes. The woman's hut was just a thatch-roofed shelter with bamboo poles and mud walls. The wind blew in through the walls and the chill would wake us up frequently. I felt nauseous all the time and thought it was the lack of food and shelter. I struggled to keep down food after every meal and certain smells were repulsive. It was actually morning sickness but I didn't know this then.

That morning, we were sitting outside the hut after tea, making plans to go out and gather herbs, when we heard a loud shout from across the hill.

It was one of the village men. Since he was on the other hill, we couldn't see him clearly but we heard him shout: 'Be careful! Some Japanese soldiers are climbing down to your hut!'

We looked at each other in shock and Aneiü began to whimper.

'Oh my God, what if they take Jimmy away!' Zhabu cried out.

'Jimmy, go and hide!' I whispered and he fled into the woods.

We could see two heavily-armed Japanese soldiers walking towards us. We quickly hid the half of Father's double barrel gun that we were carrying with us. The other half was with my brother. We left everything behind in the trench except for the cash we were carrying – about eight thousand rupees – and ran to join the woman and her children. The three of us smudged ash and mud on our faces and sat down beside the woman.

As an afterthought, I picked up one of the children and sat him on my lap. He sat there very quietly, he didn't cry, did not even struggle. These children had heard and seen so much of the war that they had lost their natural laughter and mischief. Zhabu lifted another one of the children onto her lap and we sat our youngest sister between us. Wrapping ourselves with torn shawls, we feigned sickness when the soldiers walked in.

They looked around the hut carefully and then sat down near the door without saying a word. We were petrified. The hut was so tiny that I could smell their musk. There was a stale whiff of dust and grease about them and they were panting from the steep climb.

Stories of Japanese atrocities hurtled through my mind. Our men who had been picked up by them were badly beaten and then tied to trees all night long while their captors slept. We had also heard stories of women being molested by them, spoken of in whispers among the elders, because rape was considered the most heinous of crimes and we knew very little of it before the Japanese came.

These men looking at us now were men of that race, and we had no idea how they were going to treat us. The soldier sitting closest to me leaned forward suddenly and peered into my face. I winced and turned away. The man laughed.

The soldiers said a few words in Japanese and the woman indicated that we could not understand. With wild gestures she tried to tell them that there was no food in the house. But they ignored her and remained sitting, talking among themselves. We didn't know how long they intended to stay. If they tried to harm us, Jimmy would be in no position to come and rescue us. If we tried to run, they might kill the children. All we could do was sit there silently.

After what seemed like an eternity, they rose to their feet and walked out, probably having convinced themselves there were no men to take away with them. They had seen that we had no food, either.

For a long time, we did not dare move. We didn't want to do anything to make them come back, so we watched them silently from the narrow view the entrance afforded us. We waited until they were out of sight. Then we got up and softly crept to the doorway and looked to see if they were coming back. By then, they had disappeared from view but we were so terrified that we spoke in whispers for the rest of the day.

That day, I acutely felt there was no place where we could be safe. How I missed my parents. How I wished Vic would come and take us away to safety.

The eighth of April also happened to be Good Friday. We had gone through one ordeal with the Japanese soldiers and we still had another to go through. We were extremely homesick and unhappy. We were simply concentrating on getting through each day with a meal inside us.

We knew it would soon be Easter Sunday and for the first time in our lives we would not be attending church. All day long we heard the sound of shelling and mortar-fire and we knew the war in Kohima had not ended. We felt even more unhappy to think we were spending this time in the woods, without proper food, and in the dangerous situation that the war posed for all of us. When would the war end? When could we go home? Aneiü would ask, but we had gradually stopped trying to give her answers.

10 APRIL

The tenth of April was Easter Sunday. We were woken early in the morning by a sudden storm. It was not yet dawn when lightning struck and thunder resounded through the woods. It was a storm like no other, terrifying in its intensity. The wind howled and broke off branches from nearby trees. The crash of falling branches and the sound of thunder were enough to freeze our hearts.

Then the rain began to pelt us, coming in easily through the thatch. The storm drowned out the sound of gunfire but we were buffeted by rain from every direction, the huge drops drenching us.

The noise of thunder and the forked lightning that seemed to come so close, threatening to hit our little shelter, made us very frightened. Aneiü began to cry and we were all in tears.

'Oh God, save us, save our souls,' we prayed for we thought the end had come.

It was a long time before the storm died down. But when morning came, the sun rose brightly and everything was calm. The terror of the pre-dawn storm seemed to have disappeared without any trace.

It was surprisingly quiet for some time and we realized that with the storm, the gunfire had also stopped. But the silence did not last long, the guns were soon firing again and bombs exploding in the direction of Kohima.

We slowly got out of the hut and dried our clothes in the weak sunshine. We had felt deserted by man and God during that awful storm. But now it was over and no one had been harmed, none struck by lightning.

Vikieü tried to comfort us. 'We will go through worse than this, let's be strong.'

She was right. We had to carry on with the process of living no matter how bleak life felt.

11 APRIL

Sam came to see us the next day. He was wearing a torn
Naga shawl and a man's kilt. He still had his Naga haircut.
He had brought us some food, but his face was ashen. I
asked him if he was sick. He said he wasn't sick but I knew
something was wrong.

We asked him about it several times until finally, he sat
down heavily and said, 'On my way here, I was chased by
five Japanese soldiers. They chased me for a few miles until
I came to a stream. There was a cave nearby and I ran in
there to hide. Losing track of me, they fired shots in my
direction and then went back. When I was quite sure they
had all gone away, I climbed out of the cave and made my
way to you.'

As he told his story, our dear brother had tears in his eyes
and we realized the terror he had been through, trying to
come to us. All of us wept, both in fear and relief. 'Please
don't go back,' we begged. But being a King's Scout, he
had to return to the British lines and do his part in fighting
the war. He did stay the night with us, though, and in the
early morning he was gone. His visits were a joyous time
for us because he brought us a little news and we had the
assurance that he was still alive. But this time when he left,
our hearts were weighed down by this story of how close he
had come to capture and certain death. It made us realize
the great risks he took to come to visit us.

An instance of happiness for us at the hut was the
unexpected return of Vikieü's husband. He had managed to
escape from the Japanese and made his way to us. He was
half-starved and covered with body lice. But he had had a
lucky escape. As a prisoner he was chained every night to

one of his captors. The slightest movement he made would wake up his captor. But one night, they chained him to a tree and he managed to escape and ran into the woods nearby. No one heard him and after some time, he made his way to Chieswema and furtively appeared in the village. There he met our relatives who told him the direction we had taken, and thus he managed find us.

14 APRIL

After Easter Sunday our food supplies ran low. Since her husband was back, Vikieü decided to leave her baby with him and go to Kohima village to scavenge for food. Her husband had brought his father with him, an old man in his seventies. Vikieü, Zhabu and her father-in-law went to the village. It was a perilous trip. Bullets whizzed back and forth on either side of them as they crossed the fields. They were almost shot at a few times because both sides were shooting at any moving object. Somehow, the three of them managed to crawl to the village.

As they came closer, they saw that the village was overrun by thousands of Japanese who had entrenched themselves in the thickly wooded lands belonging to the Tsieramia clan. Shells relentlessly dropped down on the village and onto the Japanese positions. But they were so close to the village that it took away their fear and they pressed on, hoping to find food in some of the abandoned houses.

When they reached the houses, they found that their journey had been in vain. The paddy in the granaries had been burnt and was unfit for consumption. There wasn't a single animal to be found, neither pigs nor chickens, for the Japanese had slaughtered and eaten everything. While they were still looking around one of the houses, a Japanese soldier came in and signalled to Zhabu to follow him. She ran back into the kitchen to Vikieü's father-in-law and grabbed his hand. Vikieü was not around as she was in another house. The old man begged the soldier to leave her alone but he picked her up effortlessly, slung her over his shoulder and walked off.

Zhabu was only fifteen but she was a sturdy young girl and very brave. She bit down on the soldier's arm till she drew blood. The soldier roared in pain and threw her to the ground.

Zhabu sprang to her feet and ran to the back door of the house where the old man was just coming out with a stick to hit the soldier. The pair ran back to the jungle footpath where they met Vikieü and they ran all the way back to our hideout without any food.

They were all badly shaken by the experience and I cried when I heard what had happened to Zhabu. After that, we gave up all hope of finding food from the village.

'There's nothing left to eat now,' said Vikieü miserably. 'Can you girls try and gather some herbs?'

We had scoured the woods nearby for herbs frequently. Zhabu and I told her, 'There's nothing, only stumps.'

She said, 'Oh, that means we haven't given the plants enough time to sprout back between gatherings.'

We cooked a little of the rice we had and ate it with salt. There was only enough left for a few more meals now.

Food was the main topic in all our conversations. We rarely talked about other things. Just food and shelter.

The next day, we had an unexpected visitor. It was Kasano, the woman who had introduced me to Vic. She had come from the Biaku camp, where many people from

Kohima village now lived. Kasano brought us a kilo of sugar and a tin of condensed milk. It was a real blessing and we were deeply grateful to the kind-hearted woman. The dispersion into the forests had hardened people and each thought only of himself. Any food procured was first shared among family members and only when it was in excess was it shared with neighbours. How different it was from what our parents and grandparents had taught us, that the better share of food was to be given to others.

When I saw Kasano, I remembered the happier times we had spent together and my first meetings with Vic and I could not help bursting into tears. I pointed out Garrison Hill to her and said, 'I'm going to walk out there and find Vic.'

She shook her head sadly and said, 'You'll never make it, no one can make it there. Be patient, it will soon be over and he'll return.'

I knew she was right and yet I felt so helpless and lonely to be away from the man I loved and to have no news of my parents, especially Mother, who was still in a dangerous war zone. We all felt terribly lonely and the beautiful golden sunset made me even more miserable. The whining of plane engines overhead, the incessant sound of shelling, these were the sounds that had become a part of our lives now. If there was a lull in the firing, we would all stop working and strain our ears, waiting anxiously for it to begin again. The shelling felt normal to us, the silence abnormal.

15 APRIL

It felt like we were always hungry these days. One morning, we found that we had no food left. Vikieü took me aside and told me, 'Aviü, you are the eldest, so I want you to decide something for the four of you. If we stay here, we will all starve to death. My husband and I have decided to move to my father-in-law's camp.'

Her words left me speechless. I had assumed that we would stick together throughout the war since we had always been sharing whatever food we found, including our rations. Suddenly, I had to be the responsible one and make decisions for everyone and I felt unready for it. What would we do now? Jimmy was still with us, he had been with us from the beginning, loyal and protective, but Jimmy was only fifteen, two years younger than I was, and I could not tell how we would fare on our own. We were all townies, not used to surviving outdoors for long periods.

I came back to my sisters and Jimmy and hesitantly told them what Vikieü had said. They were quiet for a long time and simply looked at each other. Jimmy was the first to break the silence.

'Let's go to Biaku,' he said. 'Kasano said my parents are there. They have left Rükhroma because it was infested with the Japs. Aviü, don't worry. This is what we will do and we can all stay together as before. I'll look after all of you.' So we left for Biaku that very day.

Biaku was a few miles from Tsiakhou, but it was not a long walk, at least it didn't seem too long because we were so excited about meeting Jimmy's parents. At Biaku, we found a large encampment of people from Kohima and met Jimmy's family and also some of our neighbours from the Mission Compound. Jimmy's mother sent two of her other sons to help build a shelter for us. The first thing we did was to dig a trench.

While we were working on our shelter, Marina came to hear that we were in Biaku. She quickly ran down to us.

'Aviü! Zhabu, Aneiü! Thank God you are safe!' she said. 'Come on, I'm taking you to my shelter.' Her husband and her eight-month-old baby were there, too. We told her all about our escape to Chieswema and the sudden flight from there.

'You are safe now,' she told us again and again. 'It will soon be over.'

There were fourteen of them in all, including her in-laws. They had dug a huge trench outside their shelter. Marina's family cooked their food in the open and slept in the trench at night. But if there were too many planes overhead, they never lit their fire outside because the smoke would draw the attention of either side and they could be mistaken for Japanese by the British and be bombed.

By now, we had learnt that the Japanese were everywhere, spread all over the jungles and drawing shellfire by their very presence.

'Eat that slowly,' said Marina as she served us hot food, and we hungrily ate all that she gave us.

'Oh, I have never eaten such delicious food before,' said Zhabu.

Marina laughed softly and said, 'It's because you have been starving.'

The next day we met Anyie Kereikieü. She and her husband had escaped from Kohima early in the battle but had not made it very far as they were on foot and neither were very fit any more.

Biaku was a large camp, almost like a little village. It was on an elevated slope. We could look across and clearly see the northern Angami villages. Some had been occupied by the Japanese. We could also see the shelling of those villages during the day. At Biaku, food was available every day though each share was quite small. Those who could herd down their cows had done so, and we ate dried meat for the first time in many days. When a cow was slaughtered, each family got a small share because it had to be divided among a large number of people.

In the evenings, the men and women would gather around and talk about the ongoing war. Some said they had given up hope that the British would win the war.

Rumours were rife at these gatherings and some men said that the British army had been routed from every direction but they were still holding out at Garrison Hill, Jotsoma and Zubza.

The men voiced different opinions. 'We have been abandoned by the British and left at the mercy of the enemy,' some of them said. I knew this was not true. By now, we could differentiate between the sound of the British guns and the Japanese guns. And I knew that the British forces were still there, fighting and defending Kohima.

17 APRIL

There were many young men who, like Sam, had joined the British troops, acting as guides, stretcher-bearers and porters for them. When we had been in the camp for a few days, these men received instructions to shift the village people and everyone hiding in the woods near Biaku to a safer place, as the British intended to bomb the area and wipe out all Japanese in the jungles near Biaku. This message went round the camp swiftly and there was a lot of activity as people dismantled their dwellings and packed the things they would need at the other camp.

On the seventeenth of April, we got up early and packed our few belongings. Then we got ready to join the long line of people moving out of Biaku. Zhabu carried the suitcase because she was the strongest of us three. Even Aneiü, our youngest, carried a small bundle of clothing. I was still very weak from my jeep accident. The injuries from my accident had begun to trouble me again because of the stressful life we had lived in the past weeks and I found it difficult even to walk. Nevertheless, I went with the others, hoping that we would find a safer place to stay.

The road we took was a small footpath that led towards the woods near Kohima. It was a steep downhill climb in places. We had been walking for five miles when Jimmy whispered loudly, 'Look, it's the British troops!'

They were heavily armed with rifles ready to fire and held grenades in their hands. They had leaves stuck on their helmets and clothes, and looked quite frightening. But when they saw us, they just smiled at us and waved us on and continued silently in a long line towards Meriema.

The relief we all felt at the sight of British uniforms was immense. We talked excitedly amongst ourselves.

'This means the entire area has not fallen into Japanese hands,' said Jimmy with a big smile.

'Yes,' joined in Marina, 'it means the British are still holding some areas in Kohima and beyond.'

Perhaps then, our loved ones were also safe somewhere, I prayed silently.

18 APRIL

It was late evening when we made camp. Having left Biaku, we found shelter in a cow-shed in the Kikhu woods. Around us stretched brown harvested fields. There would be no grain here. Exhausted from the lack of food and proper sleep, we made makeshift beds and settled in. But to our horror, we suddenly realized that the shed was in an exposed field with hardly any jungle cover nearby. Both sides were exchanging mortar fire, now much closer to us. Bullets whizzed past. After a sleepless night, we woke up at dawn to move to the other side of the woods.

While we were collecting our things, a lone bee suddenly came buzzing and humming and headed directly for me. It tried to settle first in my hair, then on my shoulder and hovered over me. I tried to swat it away. Then it came right in front of my face and kept buzzing there. We tried to chase it away but it kept returning to me.

'What's wrong with that bee?' cried Marina, swatting it. The bee went away for a while and then came back to me. It buzzed around me for so long that everyone was alarmed. Our people always noticed unusual signs in the natural world.

I suddenly felt alarmed and frightened. Was this bee trying to tell me something? Bringing me a message, perhaps? Our people say that if a bee does not leave off bothering a person for a long time, it is because it has a message for the person. My heart went out to Mother and Vic – had something happened to them? Was the bee trying to tell me that Mother had been killed? And Vic? Where was he now? Still at Garrison Hill or had he moved away to Dimapur?

Tears streamed down my face and I tried hard to fight them. I could not understand why I was weeping so uncontrollably, and I rushed to the back of the shed and tried to calm down. I was still sobbing when my sisters found me.

'What is it? Why are you crying?' they asked. I felt that as the oldest, I should try to be the brave one, yet here I was, crying, unable to stop. When I couldn't reply, my sisters began to cry, too. After fleeing Kohima, we were always on the verge of tears. We were so overcome by the hardships we had recently endured and the uncertainty of meeting our parents and brother again, the uncertainty of life itself now. But the incident with the bee was the final straw for me. All my fears for Mother and Vic came rushing in and I was certain that something terrible had happened to Vic.

Marina found the three of us and tried to console us. 'You mustn't cry like this. We will all go back to Kohima very soon. The British are winning the war now.'

'It's not that,' I tried to explain, but I couldn't say anything more and simply pointed to the bee, which was still hovering nearby. It continued to come after me again and again, for what seemed like hours. I was very certain something really awful had happened somewhere that would affect me. The bee never tried to sting me and it did not trouble any of the others. Finally, just as suddenly as it had come, it left me and flew off. I felt very desolate and could not forget the experience no matter how hard I tried. I joined the others but felt uneasy all day long.

After that strange incident, we left the shed and went to the Dzüpri field where Marina and her in-laws had a paddy field. Here, the mortar sounds from Jotsoma and Zubza were louder than ever. There were no trees left around us. Only the stumps of shelled trees. The very ground shook constantly with the mortar fire. We realized we were much closer to the sources of firing, and closer to the battle zones, and therefore in greater danger for our lives. Bullets flew over our heads and all around us. But we had reached a

stage where we didn't really care whether we died of a
Japanese bullet or a British bullet.

Immensely tired, sick and starving, all we wanted was
for everything to come to an end. From the fields we could
see Garrison Hill in the distance. The thick forest cover
had now burned away and there a few leafless trees dotting
the hill. Colourful parachutes hung from the branches of
some of the trees. The slopes of Garrison Hill looked as
though they had been burnt for rice cultivation, so bombed
were they. I thought of Vic and his friends and prayed for
their safety.

25 APRIL

The next day we camped at another hut. It was in the
valley and there were trees surrounding it, so we felt safer
there. Marina was with us and it was such a comfort that
she was around. We were about five miles from the first
shed. Opposite us was the Kohima–Dimapur highway. We
could no longer see Kohima from where we were. Marina
went looking for food and soon we heard her voice from
somewhere nearby: 'Jimmy, here's a papaya tree, come and
help me pluck some!' They managed to climb up and get
two fruits but they were not yet ripe, and were bitter and
quite tasteless, even to us in our half-starved condition.

We were now about three miles from Kohima. The
sounds of battle were so close that we felt ourselves to be in
the thick of the war itself. I wished I could take my sisters
and go away somewhere, anywhere, so long as it was away
from the present suffering and the deaths all around, away
from the constant echo of gunfire. Human life seemed so
meaningless in the face of war. I felt nauseated at the sight

of fresh blood on wounded men, their bandages soaked
through. We had seen so much in such little time.

Walking along the hilly jungle paths, we often came
across wounded soldiers being carried on stretchers. Those
who could walk did so, slowly stumbling along behind
their comrades with the help of bamboo staffs. It broke our
spirits to see these soldiers. In all our years under British rule
we had always looked upon the British army as invincible.
How powerful the Japanese must be if they could inflict
such terror upon the British! The wounded soldiers looked
helpless and vulnerable, many of them were not much older
than we were.

It felt like ages since we had had a bath and proper sleep.
We were filthy and our clothes were torn. The next day, just
as the sun was coming out, we went to a nearby stream to
have a wash. The stream flowed down to the bottom of the
valley. We stood above the valley and scooped up water
and washed ourselves. Suddenly we saw movement below
us. It was a long line of British troops climbing up towards
us from the valley below. Leading them was a stocky young
man, brown-skinned, dark-haired, in a shirt and shorts. One
of his legs was bandaged. We recognized him and ran down.
Zhabu and Jimmy shouted out, 'Sieso! Sieso!' The young
man leading the troops was Sieso, one of our relatives from
Kohima, and he was guiding the B-Company, heading for
Zievo Badze, the high school area, where there was a large
army camp. How relieved we were to find him.

Sieso gave us news that warmed our hearts. We had
been isolated for so long and our only source of news had
been the inaccurate rumours circulating around the camp.
Sieso told us: 'The British army never left Kohima. They are
still there, fighting for every bit of land, receiving constant

coverage from artillery batteries at Jotsoma and Zubza.' He added that reinforcements were being sent to Garrison Hill and to the northern areas of the Angami region. We found out the conditions of the roads from Sieso. He said it was safe to travel towards Jotsoma and warned us not to go back to Kohima. After meeting Sieso, we were even more homesick for Kohima and longed to see Mother and find out where Father was.

Jimmy was now reunited with his parents but he often came to see us. We told him we wanted to go back home and see Mother, and the dear boy said he would come with us. He went back to tell his parents and when he returned, he had his sister Marlene with him. How excited we were that they could both come. It was almost as though we were going on one of our picnics again! It felt like old times, except, of course, that Vic was not here. Jimmy and Marlene were carrying a small bundle each, with a change of clothes.

'Can't Marina come with us?' asked Aneiü and she ran to ask her. Marina's in-laws allowed her to accompany us, so there were six of us that day, trekking through the jungle, making our way towards Jotsoma.

We came across Angami men working as guides for the British army. They were men from our tribe and they had several wounded soldiers with them, some with their arms in slings, others with blood-soaked bandaged heads, and others still limping along with the help of bamboo staffs. A few men were borne on stretchers and carried by men from Khonoma village. The Angami men guiding and carrying the wounded soldiers each had a sharp dao on his waist belt. Some of them carried the rifles of the wounded men. Though some of the Angami men were from Kohima, there were two from Meriema, the village neighbouring Chieswema.

This was the second group of wounded soldiers we had seen. Yet, in spite of their injuries, the men waved to us and spoke words of encouragement as we approached them. They told us: 'Walk as far from us as possible, it's dangerous for you to be near us because we could be attacked at any time. But don't worry, you'll soon be safe. Carry on.' The Angamis accompanying them told us they were anticipating enemy ambushes.

We lagged behind and let them go ahead of us. Soon, we lost sight of them. After a while, we came to a footpath that took us down to the Dzüdza river. From there, the path led us up another hill. We had just begun this steep climb when there was a terrible explosion and a deafening boom. The sound had come from above us and we looked up to see a plane in flames, thick black smoke swirling around it. It disappeared from view within seconds. We were shaken but we had been through so much already, nothing would stop us now.

Before sunset, we reached the Kohima–Dimapur road. We were encouraged by our progress and picked up speed, so we managed to reach Jotsoma village by evening. Jotsoma was full of British, Indian and Gurkha troops. They were camping in the village and on the outskirts of it. Anti-aircraft guns were set up at strategic points and one gun was positioned in the direction of Kohima.

At Jotsoma, we were greeted by Mother's uncle. 'Hou, my children, how wonderful that you have reached here safely,' he said as he took us home to his family. They welcomed us and gave us chicken broth and hot rice to eat. The food tasted wonderful after our half rations of rice and herbs for the last many days. When she had made sure we were all right, Marina returned to her family. She would walk back the same way we had come to rejoin her family at a new camp, closer to Zubza.

We were given hot water to bathe in. Then we borrowed clean clothes and shoes to wear. It felt wonderful to be in Jotsoma, far away from the threat of the Japanese and in the vicinity of a well-armed and friendly army. There was very little sign of damage in the village. The houses stood safely and food was plentiful. From Jotsoma we could look down upon Kohima and see that there was still smoke rising from the village area.

We went around the village and chatted with the troops and they gave us tinned milk, corned beef and sardines from their rations. When they learnt that we had come from the north of Kohima, they took us to their senior officers and we repeated our story to them. They asked us many questions: Did we see any Japs? Did they harm us? Where and how many were there? We tried to answer their questions and gave them all the details we remembered. Like most other Nagas, we wanted the British to win the war and chase the Japanese out of our land as soon as possible because our few encounters with them had shown us how ruthless they were.

May 1944

By now, we were comfortably settled in at Jotsoma. But we felt uneasy. We still had no idea where Vic and Mother were. We would have to find the two of them and then make our way to Shillong to find Father. There were many British troops at Jotsoma and we searched the faces of the soldiers in case Vic was among them. A few times, Marlene and I ran towards soldiers who looked like Vic from afar but when we drew near, it always turned out to be a stranger. We looked eagerly at any truck or jeep passing by, expecting it to be driven by Vic.

We had been staying in Jotsoma for a week when we decided that it was futile to remain there any longer. Certainly food was readily available but food was now the least of our worries. We had no news of Mother, Father and Vic. In Jotsoma, we learnt that many of the district commissioner's staff were in Dimapur, helping the army. I wanted to leave for Dimapur at once but Jimmy thought it would be better if he went alone first. He left the next morning and we waited impatiently all day for him to return.

It was late in the evening when Jimmy returned to the village. As soon as we saw him we waved and called out to him. But he looked tired and sad. Strangely, he did not respond to our smiles and waving, which was quite uncharacteristic of him. In all the years that I had known him, Jimmy had always been cheerful, and in the ordeal we shared in the jungle, it was he who had kept our spirits up.

At first I thought he was playing a trick on us. But he drew near and said heavily, 'I have sad news, but I'll tell you all after supper.' He was genuinely disturbed and looked very helpless. The war had made him a man prematurely. But now, burdened with his news, he looked young again. It reminded me that he was only fifteen.

We refused to wait till supper to hear his news. Badgered by all four of us, he broke down and said he had met Mr Z. Angami, one of the district commissioner's officers, in Dimapur. With tears in his eyes, Jimmy looked at me and said, 'Vic was killed on the eighteenth of April by a sniper's bullet.'

My world collapsed at his words. Vic dead! Vic killed by a sniper's bullet... the news sank in slowly. I wanted to scream – but a choked cry was all that came out of my throat. Then we were all in one another's arms, sobbing uncontrollably. Jimmy's words echoed in my head again and again. Vic killed on the eighteenth of April – that was the same day that the bee had hovered around me for hours.

Everything hurt so much inside me. I felt as though my heart was going to burst from the pain, and I hoped it would. This could not be happening. Vic had said he would come back to me. He had promised. He had always kept his promises in all the time I had known him. Maybe Jimmy had made a mistake, maybe Mr Z had made a mistake;

after all, there were so many soldiers, they could easily mistake one for another.

I clung to whatever explanation I could conjure up. Part of me knew it must be true and the other part refused to believe it. Perhaps the doubting part helped me survive. I wept and wept for Vic and I also longed to come upon him by some miracle. Oh God, how difficult it was to bear this last blow. After everything we'd been through, we had hoped to find each other again and be granted happiness. This was so unexpected, none of us could accept it.

I think I may have finally fallen asleep from exhaustion though I don't remember sleeping at all. Numb and helpless, I lay in bed, staring at the roof and walls, my eyes full of tears and my body spent with all the crying. The next morning we packed and left. I did not want to stay a day longer at a place that had given me so much relief and promise of happiness, only to snatch it away without warning.

Having thanked our hosts, we walked to the main road and waited for a lift. Jimmy had found out that Father was still in Shillong, where he had been sent to carry important government papers away from the battle zone of Kohima. We decided to go to Shillong and join him. At the bridge before Zubza, the military policeman halted a truck for us and the sergeant who was driving said he would take us till Dimapur, the railway head. The main railway station was at Dimapur from where we could travel by train to Gauhati and then take a bus to Shillong.

The roads were full of British soldiers. I still could not believe that Vic was gone and I began to look at the soldiers walking past, thinking that Vic might suddenly appear and we could be together again. In my eyes, every man in olive green, with his hat partially hiding his face, looked like Vic.

I stared till they came close, only to be disappointed each time. The Royal Engineers sergeant driving the truck wore the same insignia as Vic and even had the same number of stripes on his sleeve but when I looked at his face it was not Vic's. I realized that I must look such a fool and tried to control myself but I could not stop hoping. Perhaps we would discover that Vic had been transferred to Shillong. Perhaps this, perhaps that. How much the heart deceives itself in order to stop feeling pain.

June 1944

I remember so clearly it was on the afternoon of the second of May when we reached Dimapur. We boarded the train to Gauhati almost as soon as we arrived. We reached Gauhati the next afternoon and then, finally, we found Father. He looked old and tired. We did not exchange a word. Each of us slipped into his arms one by one and we cried and cried, as though this deluge of tears would take away all the hurt and suffering. After a while, he asked about Mother, Sam and his wife, and Vic. We told him how we were separated when the Japanese came. He saw that our clothes were almost in rags and he bought some dress fabric and gave it to the tailor.

Father took us to his house and fed us good meat. But it was tasteless to me. I had no appetite for anything any more. Father rented a bigger bungalow for us, as his house was too small, and we all lived there together for a month. Though he was relieved at finding us alive, we could see that he was not at rest with no news of Mother. We did not dare tell each other this, but deep down we believed that we might never see Mother again.

It was now June and the monsoons had set in. Everyone longed to go back home but most of the houses had been burnt in the bombing of Kohima. Meanwhile, Father was planning to take us back to Kohima to search for Mother. It was at this time that orders came for him to return to Kohima. We quickly packed and climbed into a truck with Father's staff and Mr Long, an officer from Burma who worked in the same department. The truck travelled slowly from Shillong and, after a long and tedious ride, halted at the Amguri Inspection Bungalow for the night. The next day we reached the railway head at Dimapur.

Dimapur was one of the busiest stations at the time. It was crowded with army transport and mixed troops – British, American, Indian and Gurkha – and civilians of every kind. On our way up, we saw Sam on the road with some soldiers. He didn't see us at first. We called out his name excitedly and ran up to him. He hugged us and we all had tears in our eyes. It felt like a miracle to find each other again. It was from Sam that we learnt Mother was well and camping near Zubza. We couldn't wait to get to Zubza and we refused to stop at Dimapur any longer. Father got another jeep for us and we drove to Zubza.

When we found Mother we were so happy. All of us clung to her and wouldn't let her go, as though we feared we would lose her again. She looked thin and frail but she smiled at us as we clung to her. Mother didn't say much. She began to weep every time she tried to speak and we simply held each other for a long time. We had been reunited after six weeks.

But our happiness was not complete without Vic. He had won over the entire family with his love and affection and he had left behind a deep emptiness that no one else could fill. Mother wept for a long time when I told her, but she also said, 'We must not forget to be grateful for the ones who were spared.' I knew she meant Sam, who had had such a miraculous escape from the Japs. We were eager to hear how Mother and Sam had been since we were parted.

Sam told us that all this time he had been working with the British troops as a guide for the Wingate Chindits. The Chindits had held off the Japanese for a long time in Burma, buying precious time for the troops in India to recoup. They were fighting in the front. After the lifting of the siege of Kohima on 19 April, the British had taken back all the areas the Japanese had occupied. In a reversal of roles, it was now the Japanese on the run. Pushed to the border of Nagaland, they retreated back on the southern road on which they had marched in so confidently, less than two months ago.

As a last resort, the British army bombed the surrounding areas in order to starve out the Japanese. The war had been drawn out longer because the Japanese had forcibly taken rice and cattle from Kohima and the villages around Kohima. Thus, after the British army had evacuated all civilians from these areas, they heavily bombed the villages where the Japanese were sheltering. Kohima, Viswema, Khuzama, Phesama and Jakhama were all bombed. We got to know through Sam that by the time the Japanese retreat started in June, the war was officially declared over.

Sieso was sent as guide with a number of army jeeps and trucks to escort the few people still hiding in Kohima town. They found several people, including Mother and her parents. Mother recalled that they were both laughing and crying at their rescue.

Sieso was Mother's nephew. He cried out, 'Anyie! Praise the Lord that you are safe!' Mother and her parents had been in hiding in my uncle Rüzhükhrie's shed. When they saw the uniforms of the British troops they came out into the open. They were put into army jeeps and brought to a safe place near Dzüza river, where there was an encampment of refugees.

Sam had been very busy with his job of leading the troops to enemy hideouts every day. Still, whenever he found time, he went to see Mother, bringing her his rations. The war left its scars on all of us. Sam's wife Bano had given birth to a boy during the evacuation. But she lost the baby. There were just too many losses.

We left for Kohima in the afternoon. By this time, vehicles were plying up and down the Kohima–Dimapur road. Armed soldiers were still patrolling the roads. We drove up to Kohima very slowly.

We could still hear gunfire in the distance. When we entered the town, we saw a few captured enemy soldiers. Surprisingly, they looked emaciated and weak and nothing like the stocky and fearless lot that we had first encountered in Chieswema. These prisoners looked defeated and miserable.

That evening, it was too dark to go anywhere else, so we stayed at a Nepali house just outside the town. It was a small house with no walls. It had been shelled until only the roof and supporting beams were left. The tin roof was full of big holes and there was no drinking water. Still, the fact that we were back in our hometown was comforting enough and helped us endure the poor shelter.

4 JUNE

The next morning we were up early, eager to go to our house. We walked through what used to be the main part of town. None of us was ready for the terrible sight of the ravaged town. Kohima, dear, dear Kohima, had changed so much from the way we remembered it. Hardly any houses were left standing. The debris of war, bombed-out houses and shelters and empty bomb shells littered the streets. We had seen war debris on our way up from Dimapur, so we were no longer shocked.

But we were not prepared for the dead bodies littering the streets. Dead Japanese soldiers lay where they had fallen, unattended and unburied. The British army was in the process of burying its dead. Whenever they found a dead soldier in British army uniform, civilians would report it to the army, who retrieved the bodies of their soldiers and gave them a proper burial.

We had never seen so many dead bodies before. True, we had seen some dead Japanese soldiers in the jungles. But there were many more bodies on the streets in the town and they lay in different stages of decomposition. None of us had the stomach for it. There were trenches dug out everywhere. We saw abandoned rifles on the street corners and fragments of mortar shells and grenades. We were warned that there were buried mines as well. We couldn't believe this was Kohima, this mess of human destruction.

There were signs of life amidst the ruins but it was not a pretty sight. In and around the town and village there were swarms of flies hovering over the dead bodies. The local men said the trenches of the Japanese soldiers were rat- and fly-infested. The number of rats and flies had gone up enormously in the last month. We killed the rats we found and buried them. Someone said we needed to breed cats as soon as possible. The war had killed off almost every domestic animal in Kohima. So it was decided that cats would be brought from Dimapur.

Everywhere we found the same scenes of destruction and we gingerly picked our way through the debris, fearful of stepping upon a mine, or worse, a corpse.

There was nothing left of our house. The corrugated iron sheets had been removed and had been used by British troops to line the stream below our house. I suppose they did that to have some shelter from the rain at night. The walls were missing and nothing remotely resembling a house was left. There were three or four wooden house posts still standing at the back of the house, yet even these were badly damaged by bombing.

The front yard, which used to be filled with flowers, was unrecognizable. Large craters had been left by the shells and there was a lot of ammunition near the house, from different-sized mortar shells to glittering rifle shots. Apart from the two big trenches we had built in 1942 when Burma was bombed, there were new dugouts all over the garden. Our big kitchen had been bombed in half. We found planks and tin on the stone wall that separated our land from Jimmy's.

In Jimmy's garden, which overlooked our kitchen, there were rows of graves with names and dates scribbled on small, hastily erected bamboo crosses. We found more graves in our garden. The names of the men and dates of their deaths were written on small slips of paper and shoved inside bottles that had been stuck into the ground near the graves, neck down.

We could not possibly stay in our house as there was no shelter left. So we moved to our cousin Kenneth's thatched house which was still standing. It was also damaged by bullets but not as badly as our house. We spent the night there, crowded into their three rooms along with two other families. The next day we would begin the arduous job of cleaning our compound, where the body of a Sikh soldier still lay unburied in one corner of the garden, his long hair flowing onto his chest and stopping above his bloated abdomen.

We began our work early the next morning by cleaning the spring well that lay just below our house. Father and Sam hired some men to clean up the rest of our compound and bury the dead Sikh soldier. The monsoons were a blessing because we did not have to suffer for water. We collected water in the empty ammo drums left behind by the army. Sam asked the army men camped near our house to remove the ammunition and shells around our house. It was only after they did this that we felt safer about moving around and trying to clean up after the men.

Within a few days, Father and Sam had built a little shed with what they could salvage of our house materials. It was a beginning and at least we now had a roof over our heads on our own land.

August 1944

It was not until August that we were able to move into the shed. Until then, we stayed in Kenneth's house and concentrated on building a proper house on the site of the old one.

On our first day in Kohima, we met Bob, Vic's old friend and roommate. He didn't have to break the news to me. As soon as I saw him, I broke down and was overcome by a fresh bout of tears. Bob tried to console me but the harder he tried, the more I cried. When I had finally calmed down, he promised to come and see me before he left for his camp. He kept his promise.

Almost every afternoon or evening he would come and spend time with our family. Bob told us about Vic's last hours, how he had died fighting bravely till the end. He said that Vic had killed at least three or four of the enemy before he was killed by a sniper's bullet. Bob tried very hard to cheer me up. But seeing him reminded me of the wonderful time we had spent together when Vic was alive, and I could not help weeping each time he came.

One day, he said rather desperately, 'Look here, Mari, I

won't come to see you any more if you are going to cry all the time. What will your parents think of me? I'd rather stop visiting than be told off by them. I can see that my presence is not helping you at all.' But we all enjoyed Bob's company. He was a large, genial man and had grown close to us during the time Vic was courting me. So I controlled myself and promised him I would not cry again.

'You should know that no man has loved a woman as much as Vic loved you, Mari, and you should live your life with that great memory,' Bob told me one evening when we were alone in the garden. 'Every day, he took out your photograph and looked at it, Mari. Every single day. He prayed for your safety. One day, there was a terrible storm and we had no shelter at all. We were both soaked to the skin. It was a few days before Easter Sunday. I found a place where we could make a small fire and dry ourselves, but Vic was frantically searching for something.

'"What is it? Hadn't you better dry yourself off first, Vic?" I asked him. "The envelope, I can't find it." He sounded desperate. "What envelope?" I questioned. He had his jacket in his right hand and was going through the pockets carefully. Finally, he looked extremely relieved as he pulled out a soaked envelope. Inside it was a photograph of you and a lock of your hair tied in a ribbon. The first thing he did was to carefully dry out the envelope and return its contents to it. "I hope she is safe somewhere, Bob, what do you think? I hope she made it to Dimapur," he said.

'I didn't know what to tell him because I knew the bombing of the surrounding villages was going on unabated. "I am sure she has been able to escape the bombings and is safe. She would be making her best effort for you, Vic," I said. By this time, we knew that many more people were being evacuated from the villages to the north. Vic told me, "I am going to get out of this and go back to her. Mari needs me now more than ever." The rest of us had our loved ones, too. We thought of them when the combat grew so close that we were fighting the Japs from our trenches. But not in the way Vic thought of you. You were a bright light in his head and he really wanted to live for you.

'The day before he died, we sat wearily in our trench, passing a canteen of water to one another at intervals. The weariness showed on Vic's face for the first time. His face was unshaven and he looked much older than his thirty-one years. But he suddenly turned to me and smiled. That smile transformed him. In a twinkling, he looked young and hopeful and it made me realize that he had not given up. We were being told every day that reinforcements were on their way. If we could only hold out for a day or two longer, it would all be over.

'The next morning, there was a Japanese sniper in a tree, picking off our men. I told Vic to be careful as he crawled out of the trench. "I will be," he said cheerily. He climbed out before me and was shot at. The shots missed him. I joined him quickly and we began shooting in the direction from which the shots were coming. There were four of us in our trench and we had all climbed out and were shooting at the enemy. Suddenly I heard a cry and saw someone fall to the ground. It was Vic. He had been shot in the forehead. He died instantly.

'Vic didn't feel any pain, Mari. There are terrible ways of dying on the battlefield, with your legs shot off or your stomach shot through. Vic had the most painless death of all. I am telling you this because you should draw comfort from it. The night before he died, he was telling me about his childhood. I know that after he met you, he was so happy and his life was fuller with you in it. He really loved you, Mari.'

Bob's voice was sad as he came to the last word. I was grateful to hear what he had told me and felt peaceful for the first time since I had found out that Vic was dead.

A few days later, Bob said he would try to take me to Garrison Hill to show me the place where Vic was laid to rest. I wanted to see the dug-out where Vic had lived, struggled and fought so bravely in his last days. Vic had been killed on eighteenth April. Had he lived one more day, reinforcements would have reached them and he might have come home safely. I felt angry at the thought that the one man I wanted to share my life with had been taken away in the last hours of battle. Ever since he left us on the third of April, Vic had been fighting alongside his mates.

Bob could not take me to Garrison Hill for a long time because men were at work there, clearing up the buried mines. It was too dangerous to venture out before they had cleared the mines from the area.

September 1944

By September my pregnancy had begun to show though it wasn't until June that I knew I was pregnant. As the days passed, the child within me grew bigger. Sometimes I felt it move and I prayed for its survival. This was all I had left of Vic: his child, our child, and I dearly wanted the baby to live. Vic had probably suspected that I might have conceived. I remembered him saying before we parted, 'If the baby's a boy name him David and if it's a girl name her after you.'

I had a difficult pregnancy. In the first three months, I had felt very weak from morning sickness. It made me miss Vic even more. Only after the period of nausea had passed was I able to eat normally. Mother comforted and encouraged me: 'We have lost a precious person but now another one is going to fill the empty place in our hearts. Be brave, eat, and try to strengthen yourself.'

She often said, 'I wish we could get some chicken so I could make some broth for you; you have all starved for too long and gone through so much. I don't want you to do anything else now but try to regain your strength.'

Mother tried to cook tasty meals out of the bully beef, salmon and sardine tins we received. She was a good cook and would add herbs and garlic to make a broth full of flavour. Or she would make a curry out of the bully beef. But nothing tasted the same any more. With a great deal of effort, I ate, remembering that I also had to eat for the baby. We were all suffering from anaemia and malnutrition from the weeks of starvation.

After a few weeks, Bob moved to a camp at the 42 milestone on the Indo–Burma road. It was some five miles from Kohima. He continued to visit us, and one afternoon, he finally took me to Garrison Hill to look for Vic's grave. We walked through the district commissioner's bungalow, crossed the tennis court and climbed up the hill. There were rifles belonging to both armies scattered everywhere. We saw the mortar shells and grenades that were yet to be cleared. With the rain setting in, the grass had grown thick and tall and we could not find Vic's grave. We went back from the cemetery dejectedly. Bob drove me home and returned to his camp.

The next week we tried again. By then, soldiers and civilian labourers had worked together to clear up the debris. The weeds and overgrown grass had been cut and the graves were neatly marked on the hill. Bob and I found a little bamboo cross bearing Vic's name and the day on which he had died. I cried a little but felt spent, as though I had already shed all the tears of a lifetime after hearing of his death.

We sat by the cross for a long, long time. The sun set behind us, its colours subdued. The skies were soft orange and mauve and soon the cicadas began to sing. The light remained for a while because it was still summertime. But soon the mosquitoes came out, so Bob and I climbed back down the hill, without saying a single word to each other.

Did life end at eighteen? At one point, I had wanted to die with Vic. I missed him terribly. I could not imagine life without Vic, because his entry into my life had seemed like the beginning of life. He had so many plans for us. But when I saw the grave and his name, I felt dull and my heart felt hollow. I had to accept that Vic would never come back to me.

And then I felt my baby move inside me, in tiny quivering movements. And that movement, even when it was the slightest, was like the tugging of life. I decided then to live, not pine away; I convinced myself that it was not treacherous to Vic's memory, that he would have wanted me to live. Sometimes it is easier to choose death to end pain, and sometimes, great love will choose life in spite of terrible pain. I chose life; I hope it testifies to the greatness of my love.

December 1944

She had her father's eyes. My baby daughter was born on the nineteenth of December on a cold winter's night. With joy mingled with grief, we greeted her into the world. We wept because she was fatherless but we rejoiced that we had been given a healthy baby, a life to replace the one we had lost. How perfect she was. Her tiny pink feet and hands were well-formed and there was soft white down on her cheeks.

Father said she must be called by the name her father had chosen for her and so we called her Marion. Father and Mother had their own special name for her: Neilano or Neilaü. 'Her name means we will be happy again,' said Mother. And we were happy but my happiness was tinged with a pain and sadness that sometimes stopped the laughter welling up in my throat at a good joke.

How difficult the sunset hours were for me in those days. The sun setting below the blue mountains would make the valley glow with varying lights and colours. On some evenings it would be scarlet. Almost everyone would stop working and come outside to watch the sun sink below the horizon like a scarlet ball. On other evenings it would be an uncertain conglomeration of dark blue and purple and orange tints.

On such evenings, I would watch that distant beauty, unable to deaden my deep longing for Vic. And I would think that somewhere, maybe, my love was watching me and could perhaps see our child; somewhere, maybe, he was longing to dandle her on his lap and do all the things a father would do for his child. How hard it was. Life had slowly returned to normal for everyone else but I had been changed by the war, never to be the same again.

By the end of 1944, all the inhabitants of Kohima returned home. This included the families that had fled to Shillong during the war years. They returned to find their houses burnt down and uninhabitable. The only houses that were left undamaged were Anie Rüzhükhrie's house, a few houses in town and the little mahogany house at the Mission Centre.

With the declaration that the war was over in our hills, the work of reconstruction began. The rest of the year was spent in building houses. Every day we witnessed the amazingly resilient spirit of our people. The building of houses became a communal activity. Neighbours got together and worked on each other's houses. The work proceeded so much faster in this way.

For several months, the steady beat of nails being hammered on beams and tin came to replace the loud bursts of constant shelling that had filled our skies during the war months. No one complained about the hammering. People were only too happy to work on the houses, going from one house to the other and checking on the progress their neighbours had made.

Right after the war, food continued to be a problem. The Japanese occupation of Kohima had attracted a lot of mortar shelling upon the village and in the last stages of the war, the Allied Air Force had resorted to a continuous bombing of the village. The bombings had started fires in several places and at one point the entire village burned for days. The abundant granaries and food supplies stored by the villagers to last the year had been burnt and there was no food that could be retrieved or was found edible. Even the few animals that survived the war refused to eat the burnt grain. The government arranged for the Assam relief fund to distribute rations, which included rice, tea, sugar and salt. The rations were to be distributed until a time when the civilian population would be able to fend for itself again.

Though the war was over, a certain tension remained for a long time – the fear of undetonated mortars and grenades. We found two-inch and three-inch mortar shells on our lands. The elders in the village cautioned people not to wander about carelessly in the ruins. They warned about the danger of being injured if the undetonated shells were to explode accidentally. The elders warned the younger boys in particular, who, they knew, would be curious about any ammunition they found. Jimmy discovered some grenades with the pins removed. They were possibly duds but there was no way to be certain. We begged him not to keep them. None of us wanted an accident to happen, not after surviving this far.

February 1945

I never thought our land would recover from the toll the war had taken on it. But when spring came, the change over the battlefield Kohima had been just a year ago was incredible. The remaining trees sprouted new leaves. Wild flowers bloomed in abundance. In the Garrison Hill area, new grass covered the ground surfaces that had been bombed and left behind shallow craters in the bombed spots.

Many of the trees had been destroyed by enemy gunfire and shelling. The stumps of these trees were uprooted and new trees planted in their place. It was as though nature was repairing the damage suffered by the earth in the previous year and the government, too, worked hard to restore normalcy to the town and village.

Mr Pawsey, the district commissioner, met the village elders and suggested that the village be levelled down with bulldozers. But the elders were outraged at this.

They told Mr Pawsey, 'Chaha, if you level the village lands, we will lose our boundary lines. The boundary lines are very important to us because they show the borders between clans. How can we distinguish between clan boundaries if you level the village? There will be terrible fights and the land disputes between clans or even between individuals could destroy the entire village.'

Mr Pawsey listened to them and finally understood that this was simply our way of doing things. So he abandoned his first plan.

The government then appointed men to list the names of those whose houses had been destroyed. Then they began to supply us with tin and timber as compensation. The damage varied from house to house but every house was damaged in some way. We cleared away the debris of war ourselves, rifles, mortar shells and other waste.

Before the war, many of the village houses had been made of thatch, so they easily caught fire from the bombing. The people retrieved half-burnt posts and erected sheds in which they lived whilst working on their new homes. After the war, everyone built houses of tin with corrugated iron roofing. Thatched houses disappeared from the village.

There was no road in the old village before the war. The villagers used the paths between the clan lands. The government decided it was a good time to construct a circular road that ran right round the whole village. It made some of the elders joke and say, 'Thank God for the war; if it hadn't come to us, we would never have got this road.'

The Angami spirit was resilient. People observed long months of mourning for their dead but got on with the business of life determinedly. There were families, other than ours, who had lost loved ones. Some of the men who worked for the British to carry ammunition had been shot at and killed by the Japanese. A young Angami soldier of the Lhisemia clan was one of the first casualties and he was buried in the war cemetery that was built soon after the war. Many people had lost their relatives to the shelling.

But once the period of mourning was over, further grieving was discouraged. 'Don't displease the spirits,' the villagers said. 'If you grieve too much, it will anger the spirits and even greater grief will come to you.' After a great calamity, our people always tried their best to keep their spirits up. That was the way of our people.

March 1945

All kinds of strange stories circulated after the war. There were rumours of Japanese soldiers in the Chakhesang villages who did not want to return when the retreat began. It was said that they disguised themselves as Naga villagers and got their hair cut in the Naga fashion. These soldiers reportedly followed the villagers to the fields and worked alongside them. Having befriended the villagers, they married women from those tribes and settled down there.

We also heard that in the southern Angami villages people returned to their homes to find paddy stalks growing in their front yards. They were from seeds that had fallen out of the bags of paddy taken by the Japanese. The villagers transplanted these stalks and eventually harvested them.

People frequently found mementos of the war – Japanese helmets and rifles and bullets. There was a lot of what was called 'Japanese money' found in houses in the villages around Kohima and in the town of Kohima. The paper notes had writing on them in English. Some said 'Government of Japan' and there were notes of 'ten rupees' or 'fifty rupees'. When the Japanese first came to the southern villages, the local people had been 'paid' with this Japanese money for their labour of carrying ammunition and providing food. The villagers soon realized the money was actually worthless, but they were still forced to labour for the Japanese.

Mr Pawsey gave strict orders for the money to be collected and burnt outside the municipal office. This was done and some of the younger boys picked out half-burnt notes from the ashes. Our people also found several guns. However, another order was quickly issued and the men reluctantly brought in the guns they had found and surrendered them to the district commissioner. The people had been duly warned that those who hid any of the guns would be heavily penalized.

Slowly, the shops reopened. The Bengali shops found a long line of customers when they opened their doors. The Marwaris, however, were not allowed to return to trade in Kohima. Mr Pawsey had cancelled their permit. The reason he cited was that they had abandoned Kohima during the war, unlike the Bengali traders who had stayed on. Mr Pawsey gave the Marwari shops to some of the Angamis instead, who wanted to become traders themselves. They took on the business and began to sell the commodities that the Marwari shops used to stock.

Neilasa was one of the first Angami shop-owners, selling carpentry tools and paint. His success encouraged others to take up the new profession of trade and commerce. For the first time, a shop selling yarn was opened on the Mission Road. The new shops focused on the goods that were most in demand, such as food items, carpentry tools, shoes and clothes. A bazaar for meat and vegetables was set up in town and it ran a thriving business from the beginning.

April 1945

In early 1945, the reconstruction work in the Kohima village and town was completed. 1944 had been a long, hard year. But now people wanted to get on with their lives. When some semblance of normalcy was restored, a few young men got together to reopen the school in the town. Neiliehu Belho and Vibeilie Belho had graduated from high school before the war. They felt sorry for the younger ones who were missing out on an education so they got the old school building repaired and began running classes from there, teaching the students themselves. Men came from Kohima village to help repair the damaged school building. Many parents were grateful for the work they had done and they sent their children to school; even Zhabu and Aneiü attended.

But in about two months, the government closed down this privately run school and appointed a teacher to reopen the Mission School in its place. In the absence of the missionaries, Lhuviniu Lungalang, one of the first Naga graduates, was appointed to look after the school with the help of other local teachers. The new teachers, Rosalind,

Putsüre and Lucy, taught alongside older teachers like Rüzhükhrie, Shürholhoulie, Duosielhou and Pfeno.

A few months later, Rev Supplee came back to Kohima. As soon as he returned, he shifted the school into the abandoned hospital premises. He also repaired the hostel buildings below our lands and used them as schoolrooms. The hospital was shifted to the Serzou colony and built as a much bigger establishment.

The Mission School had always been a government-run school. We were very glad when it reopened because my sisters could continue with their education properly. The Mission School became a high school and was upgraded to include classes seven to ten. This was a big relief to many parents. Now Aneiü and Zhabu, and their friends, would not have to go to Shillong to finish high school. Although the two men had done a good job by reopening the school, it wasn't officially recognized by the government. So it was a relief to get the government school running again so that students could get a proper degree.

The school building had been badly damaged in the war. Many rooms were destroyed and took a long time to repair. While the repair work was going on, our uncle Rüzhükhrie, who was also the maths teacher, often took his students to his house and taught them there rather than waste a day of teaching.

Aneiü always had stories to tell when she came home from school. Theirs was a boisterous class. As the youngest in the family, she was mischievous by nature and she and her friends would play tricks on their teachers.

Mother scolded her a lot one day when Aneiü recalled something she and her friends had done at school for which they had been punished.

'Mother! We were only having some fun together, what is so wrong about that?' Aneiü protested. They had been caught putting glue on the teacher's seat!

Mother warned her that their tricks could be misinterpreted. The truth was that my sisters and their friends were thoroughly enjoying going back to school. It increased the sense of normalcy that had been taken away by the war.

Zhabu was far more sensible than her younger sister and a level-headed student as well. Zhabu was also the healthiest among the three of us. She enjoyed working in the fields and joined other young people of her age when they went to till each other's fields. Mother took Zhabu with her when she gathered wood from the forested land we owned on Bayavü Hill. At sixteen-and-a-half, she was able to work as hard as a grown person.

Aneiü, however, was a weakling. She was small at birth and very sickly. So Mother did not like to let her work as hard as the older ones. Still, when she insisted on accompanying Zhabu to the fields, she was given a child's carrying-basket to use. At least she got on well with her lessons at school.

I envied them their carefree minds. When they laughed together, I could not always join in. I couldn't help but feel that I had been completely transformed by the war. I had bidden farewell to childhood and I could not find it again.

May 1945

My new life as a mother took up all my energy. During the day, my baby kept me busy. She had to be fed and bathed and have her diapers changed every few hours. There was so much to do and with a baby around there was never a moment's rest. I felt happy to do all this because it kept me from brooding over the past, and I loved my baby so dearly I felt like I couldn't do enough for her. Father and Mother helped to look after her and my younger sisters were happy to babysit as she grew bigger.

Marion was very little trouble as a baby, and at four months, Mother said she could be fed solids so we alternated her diet between breast milk and some fruit or softly-boiled rice. It worked wonders for her and she grew rapidly, her little arms and legs growing stronger every day.

Our female relatives from the village often visited and gave me advice on looking after Marion. I learnt to oil my baby before bathing her. It would give her strong limbs, Anyie Kereikieü had explained. I learnt to strap her to my back and carry her while I did the housework. It was tricky at first and I frequently asked Mother to help put my baby on my back but after a week, I managed to do it on my own.

I never had much time now to think about what I should do with my life. At night we both fell into an exhausted sleep, mother and child, and I was grateful for this because I had spent so many nights sleepless, sobbing quietly into my pillow, afraid to wake anyone but unable to hold back my tears. Now I had a reason to live. My baby needed me. After months of listlessness, my appetite returned and it pleased Mother to see me eat much larger portions than during my pregnancy.

The days went by rapidly. On 18 April, I had taken flowers to Vic's grave. It now had a headstone that bore his name and regiment and the cemetery was neatly arranged in long rows of graves. When Bob had taken me the first time, the graves were makeshift wooden crosses. Now they had bronze plaques with the men's names written on them. The army had removed the Lee tank that had crashed into the tennis court during the battle. It was now kept just beside the highway where the government planned to preserve it as a reminder of the war. With all the mines cleared and gravel laid over the walkways, the cemetery looked peaceful, as it should.

Paper poppies brought by parents and widows fluttered over the graves. It was a sight that brought fresh tears to my eyes. Flowers bloomed in the corners where they had been planted – tea roses, Michaelmas daisies and some amaryllises. My dear one was gone from me. I felt the finality of his death whenever I visited his grave and saw his name afresh. But we had our child, a beautiful testament to our love, and I resolved to take care of her as best as I could, and be both mother and father to her.

By this time, much of the rebuilding work in the Kohima village was nearing completion. Mr Pawsey and his men had been very busy the first few months, distributing building material to those whose houses had been destroyed by the shelling. Around the same time, a bulldozer worked continuously on the village road. With the road built right through the village, it looked better than ever. The ruins of the wartime village had been cleared away. It was a very good thing, said Father, because many whose lands were taken in the road building received compensation. The church was one of the first buildings to be restored.

Before the reconstruction work began, Father said to his cousin, 'Rüzhükhrie, we must build the church first.'

My uncle replied, 'Man, are you mad? You don't have a house to shelter your family and you are saying we must build the church first? Hielie, are you serious!'

But Father was adamant. 'We must build the house of the Lord first.'

So these two buildings were built at the same time, our house and the village church. This church eventually became too small for the worshippers. When a new church was constructed in 1954, the old church area was turned into a graveyard.

Father and Sam built the new house to resemble our former house very closely. It had a foundation of stone about two-and-a-half-feet high. The rest of the house was built of strong beams and timber. On the west wall, Father had placed aluminium sheets, which were cheaper than tin but made a hissing sound at night. The bathroom had a cemented floor. We also rebuilt the outhouse in the back garden. We began to tend to the gardens once more and Mother slowly refilled her garden with vegetables and herbs.

June 1945

When Zhabu and I began to plant flowers again we found our land still strewn with bullets. We found bullet casings each time we dug up a new flower bed. There must have been a lot of fierce fighting on our land after Mother left the house. We spent hours collecting the bullets and remains of shells. Father and Sam took away some undetonated grenades that we found and warned us about mines. Fortunately, there were none. We found many empty artillery casings, though.

Jimmy and his parents were some of the lucky ones who found their house still standing. Of course, much of it was badly damaged but the main posts still stood and their house needed less work than ours did. They were able to settle into their house before us.

There was an empty plot of land behind our house and Father's friend Kumbho came to build his house there. He and his wife, Aunt Aiti, had nine children – three girls and six boys. The two youngest boys were a few years younger than Aneiü. We made friends with them easily. Thus our neighbourhood was peopled again and life returned to a semblance of what it used to be before the war.

Many of our relatives in the village of Kohima had new houses by now, and they resumed their work in the fields. In the summer months we saw new grain in the fields once again and the familiar landscape of young paddy and newly green trees returned to Nagaland.

There were more tin houses than thatched houses in the village now. On the outskirts of the village, the new houses were mostly painted white or yellow with red roofs, making them look neat and pretty. It was as though the war had never happened. I felt almost angry at life in these moments. My own life had been turned upside down by the war. And the way everything around me had returned to normal so quickly seemed unfair.

Most of the British troops had left within a few months of the war and dear Bob left with them. There were some new troops posted under the district commissioner to help build the war cemetery and assist in re-establishing the administration. It was still a common sight to see British soldiers in their trucks and jeeps, driving around Kohima. I had long stopped looking for Vic and felt much older than the rest of my friends, who spoke excitedly about the new troops in town and joined them on walks and picnics.

One evening, there was a loud knocking on our door. It was growing dark but you could still distinguish faces in the half light. I hurried to the door and was surprised to find four young soldiers outside. The first one stammered a little and asked if I could show them to Jimmy's house as they had forgotten the way. I led them out and up the short path that lay between our house and Jimmy's.

Both Jimmy and his sister Marlene were at home and they greeted their friends warmly. I came back to my house as I had to put Marion to sleep. The next evening, I was in the garden adjoining Jimmy's land when I heard the sound of laughing young voices carried over by the wind. I thought nothing of it and continued to pluck the sour herbs that Mother liked to add to her delicious broths.

The sudden sound of running feet startled me. I turned to find one of the soldiers from the evening before. He had jumped over Jimmy's fence and was running towards me. I was surprised. I didn't know what to think, really, but I reasoned that he must be taking a short cut through our land because he was late reporting for duty. But he came up to me, caught my hands in his and began to say, 'You are so beautiful, I beg you to go out with me. Please don't say no.'

I shrank back in fear. A muffled little scream escaped me.

He let go of me instantly, took a step backwards and apologized. 'I'm sorry, I didn't mean to scare you, I only wanted to let you know how much I like you.'

I calmed down a little.

'I'm Jimmy's friend, Dickie. We were here last night, don't you remember?' he asked.

I said I did.

'Come out with me tomorrow, please,' he pleaded.

I blushed and held my head low, unable to bear the gaze of his admiration. Then I said, 'I can't go out with you. Please go now.'

He looked disappointed but said, 'Please don't be angry.' He was very young and looked piteous as he stood there with his cap in his hands, asking me to forgive his impetuousness.

'I'm not angry, but you had better go,' I said.

'What's your name, can you at least tell me that?' he asked.

'Mari,' I said in a low voice.

It was so low I doubted that he had even heard, but he had and he blurted out, 'What a sweet name, Mari! Mari, I will see you tomorrow then?'

I shook my head.

'May I keep trying, Mari?' he asked, looking at me hopefully.

I didn't have the heart to say no again but I didn't say yes either.

The whole incident could not have lasted more than five minutes but I was so affected by it I had to sit on a grassy knoll and try to quiet my beating heart. I was very uneasy about the encounter. I felt a strange stab of guilt as though I had been untrue to Vic. I suppose in a way I had. A little. I had not stopped loving Vic and it felt treacherous to his memory. In my mind, he was still my husband and I wanted it to remain that way.

I certainly didn't want to develop feelings for someone for whom I could be just a passing fancy. I did not believe I could find another man who would love me the way Vic had, so completely. Just then, I heard Mother calling out to me, so I suppressed my thoughts and ran down to her with the sour leaves.

'Aviü, what a long time you have been in the garden – is this all that you could bring back? I will have to cook something else, this is too little for a meal,' she chided me.

It made me feel guilty again because Mother and Father had both been so good to me over the past months, silently sharing my loss of Vic and never pressing me into hard work.

August 1945

After that day, the young soldier sent me messages thrice through Jimmy, asking to meet. I didn't respond. I felt confused and unsure. I could not understand why the encounter had disturbed me. He was the smartest of the four soldiers who had come to our house. He was young too, very young, certainly much younger than Vic – and that worried me. It was almost as though he was a young Vic, returning to me again; the impetuous way in which he expressed his feelings, his admiration, was just like Vic.

After a few days, my friends urged me to go out with them. Marlene came to tell me that their new friends would be there too. But I hesitated. I didn't want to make another mistake. Not that Vic had been a mistake but I feared the pain of loss and parting too much.

That night, I lay awake while my child slept on, missing Vic dearly and reliving the days we had shared together. After tossing and turning for a long time, I got up and took out the engagement ring Vic had given me. I slipped it on my finger, as though willing it to protect me.

In the weeks that followed, Dickie, the young soldier,

kept sending messages through Jimmy and Marlene. They told me, 'He really likes you and he's a nice guy.'

His real name was Richard Harris but everyone called him Dickie. He was a captain in the army. When he sent a fourth invitation, I finally relented and went to a party with him.

It was a small gathering of people I already knew – Jimmy and Marlene and the three soldiers who had accompanied Dickie. The one named Harry was quite friendly. The other two, Lou and Peter, were a little shy. Harry played some records for us. Later in the evening, some more people joined us and we played games and laughed when we made mistakes. Before dinner, Dickie took me aside.

'Ah, Mari, I am in love with you,' he said. He looked so sincere when he said that. My mind protested against it but my heart felt moved to hear his words. I thought then that perhaps life does not have to be so painful after all. I told him about Vic though he had already heard my story from Marlene and Jimmy.

Dickie was gentle and understanding. I don't think I would have liked him if he were not so gentle. The party was soon over and he dropped us back, saying he would come to see me again.

Dickie and I got to know each other better in the autumn, spending time together, talking about things that were important to us both. Though Dickie was a soldier, just like Vic had been, we were living in different times now with the war behind us. The anxiety that Vic and I had known was no longer there. Dickie and I had more time for each other.

He understood that I felt confused about my feelings for him and that made me trust him more.

'Take all the time you need, Mari, I'll wait for you,' he would say. 'I'm just so grateful to be with you.'

Shyly at first, I talked to him about life and wanting to give my child a safe home to grow up in.

'I'd like to be part of that home,' he said softly.

We began to go out frequently, driving out to a knoll that overlooked the Kohima–Dimapur highway. Sometimes his friends, Harry, Lou and Peter came with us and we took picnic baskets along. The outings brought back memories of the times I had spent with Vic. At first, it felt odd. Things had changed so much since then.

These young men were among the last soldiers to leave Kohima. Their job was to look after the war graves. Every Sunday, they came to attend the service in English at the Mission church.

It had been a year since the American missionary couple, Reverend and Mrs Supplee, were back in Kohima. They were very fond of Dickie and his friends. The young soldiers would come to church in a big group with Mr Pawsey. Sitting in church while Rev Supplee boomed out his sermons, Dickie and his friends would surreptitiously steal glances down our row. Lou played the piano well and often played after the service. After church, they always lingered behind and chatted with the Supplees and the choir boys. The missionaries were particularly fond of the young men because they shared a mutual love of music.

December 1945

In December, Marion turned one. I sewed her a new dress and we invited our friends to celebrate her birthday. Jimmy and Marlene were both there and we spent the whole day together. Little Marion was the centre of attention as she toddled back and forth, walking short distances and falling on her bottom. She soon grew tired of it and fell fast asleep. We put her to bed and then ate dinner. Dickie and his friends came too, with gifts for Marion.

Dickie and I were growing closer every day. He took me out for drives in his jeep whenever he could. And my affection for him grew steadily. I think my love for Dickie was tinged with hope. It was like turning away from the sad abyss that was the past to embrace a sweeter future.

'We are children of the war,' he once said to me with a serious look on his face. 'We have to grab life and love when we find it and hold onto it fiercely.'

I suppose that was what we did. Fearfully at first, but after that, with renewed hope. Every day I cherished life anew. Dickie's love gave me reason to. He had said often enough that he wanted to marry me and I had no reason to doubt him.

Dickie loved music. He was a clarinet player but he could not play in Kohima as he did not have his instrument with him. To compensate, he had a record player and lots of records. One of his favourite songs was 'My blue heaven'. We would sing along to it and instead of 'Just Molly and me and Baby makes three' he would sing 'Just Mari and me and Wavell makes three'. Wavell was his large black dog that he had irreverently named after Field Marshall Wavell. All the other soldiers liked Dickie because he had a great sense of humour. 'What a bloke!' his friends would call out when he had made some outrageous joke.

But when he was alone with me, he showed me his serious side, and told me about his own life. He wrote often to his parents, who were in England, and he was very attached to his mother. He wrote to her almost every day and received many letters from her, too. Dickie had joined the army soon after the war broke out, when he was only eighteen. He first served in north Africa where he was wounded in a hand grenade attack. After that, he was transferred to India and eventually came to Nagaland. Dickie was first posted in the eastern part of Nagaland, at an army post in Wakching, which he described as 'a page out of *National Geographic*' because it was so scenic. When the war ended, he was posted in Kohima.

Dickie was at heart a very affectionate and caring person. But only those close to him got to see the softer, romantic side of him. I knew other women found him attractive. He would sometimes get letters from a woman in the military nursing services. Her name was Sheila. She wrote him page after page, asking him to marry her. Often she would ask if he still loved the Naga girl he was seeing. I felt sorry for her; I knew how she felt because Dickie was by far the best-looking soldier in these parts.

I felt lucky to be Dickie's girl. He was very handsome, with clearly defined features and wavy brown hair. When he was in a good mood, his eyes sparkled mischievously. When we were alone, he would say every now and then, 'I love you, Mari, don't leave me.'

I was sure Dickie loved me truly and would look after me. We both knew there would be many obstacles when we got married but we were happy to take the present for what it had to offer. And in that present, we were happy to be alive and in love. He spoke of taking me back to England as his bride but that was still a long way off.

There were many evenings when Dickie would play football, taking me along to watch him play. He played well and was vibrant and full of life. Football was the most popular game in Nagaland. On some Saturdays, the Third Assam Rifles, Dickie's team, played against the Naga Club. On other days, they would play against the Mission School boys.

These were days of peace now and people wanted to forget the painful memories of the war so there was a lot of social activity. While the older people were preoccupied with rebuilding the village of Kohima and normalizing life in the town, the younger people just wanted to catch up on the things they had missed out on.

February 1946

How quickly the tension of the war years disappeared. But in our hills the peace was uneasy. Things were moving rapidly. Father and his friends were frequently in deep conversation about the political changes that would soon take place. The British government was moving out, they said, and India and Burma would become independent countries.

I was only mildly curious about these things. But I grew alarmed one day when Dickie spoke of leaving India. Mr Pawsey was still administering as district commissioner of the Naga Hills. But we heard he would leave as soon as the procedure for Indian independence began. Dickie worked directly under Mr Pawsey, who was a stern administrator, known to all for his integrity and strict ways. For Dickie and the other British soldiers, Mr Pawsey was a father figure and his word was law. The younger men were in complete awe of him and he commanded the same response from the local people.

Dickie and I had been together for about seven months when I became pregnant again. I was more scared than happy because I foresaw a long struggle before me. I hoped we would be able to get married soon. Dickie was thrilled about the idea of us having a child together, but I was worried about the future. I knew that Dickie would have to leave too, if his superior officer left. Dickie sought Father's permission to take me back to England as his wife but Father and Sam were unwilling to let me go. Sam cautioned me: 'Aviü, he is very young. I want to be sure he can look after you. I don't want you to get hurt again.'

It was true that Dickie was much younger than Vic and he had not become a part of my family the way Vic had. Dickie was shy and unsure of how he would be received. When he visited, he sat formally in the living room and my parents were formal with him too, always courteous but unable to get onto the familiar ground they had shared with Vic. I felt it was unfair to Dickie to compare him with another man but in a way it was inevitable. My family loved me dearly and, having seen me go through so much pain, they were extremely protective of me.

Our last days together were sad and short. We both knew we had to part. Whenever he took me out, we simply sat on our knoll, holding hands, not speaking for long periods of time, each lost in our own thoughts.

One afternoon, he came to the house, looking very sad.

'What's wrong?' I asked.

'I'm sorry, Mari, I have received my transfer orders. I have to leave for Silchar soon.'

My heart sank within me.

'When?'

'In another two days.'

I cried and he held me in his arms and kept saying over and over again, 'I'm sorry, Mari, I'm so sorry.'

But there was nothing either of us could do about it. He

had to leave for Silchar with the rest of his regiment. He promised to return for my delivery. I felt very abandoned and unsure. Would he come back? I was not certain. I stayed home as much as I could. It was all I could do to get through each day.

When there were just a few days left, Dickie took a few days' leave and returned and I gave birth to a lovely baby girl. Dickie named her Lily. Our baby looked so much like her father, her tiny features resembling Dickie closely. I was happy for Marion that it was a girl, a little playmate for her. But the second pregnancy was harder on my family. Vic and I had been accepted as a married couple. He had been my husband even though we had not been married by the church. But not Dickie. He never became my husband in the manner that Vic did. My family had trouble accepting my relationship with Dickie and we had even exchanged harsh words on that account.

After my baby was born, we went to the village council, as was the custom, and registered the child. After this, both my children were acknowledged as the legal offspring of their fathers. This was how a foreigner was accepted by and adopted into a tribe. Now the children had the right to settle in the land of their birth and own property if they chose to.

I had a difficult decision to make now. Should I leave for England with my daughters and Dickie and make my home there? Dickie was still offering me that choice. Or should I stay? I knew that if I left, I would not be able to come back and see my parents and my brother and sisters for a long time. We had never been parted before. The separation during the war months had been terrible, especially as we did not even know if we would meet again.

I was still young and innocent of the outside world. I wanted to be with Dickie but didn't feel brave enough to leave home. Could I bear to be parted from Dickie? It had been such torment when Vic died. But could I leave my family behind?

Just around that time, Mr Pawsey sent word that he would not allow Dickie to stay behind in Kohima nor take his small family with him to England, and Dickie felt pressured to do as he was told. I had to reluctantly agree with him. I could not leave my parents and my family at this time. I was too young.

When he finally left, I thought I would die from the heartbreak. Vic was dead and gone so I knew he would never return to me. But to have Dickie wrenched from me while we were both still living seemed harder to accept than the parting from Vic.

Dickie promised to write as soon as he was back in England but he never did. In the days and months and years that followed, I would think of him every day, wondering if I had made the wrong decision in choosing to stay behind. I had no idea where he was now. As the months passed, our daughter grew up slowly and soon began to walk. Then one day, I realized with shock that it had been two years since Dickie had left. I thought he must be back in England by now. Perhaps he had married someone else. The thought was unbearable and I pushed it aside each time.

The loneliest moment of my day was at sunset. My sisters would call me to come out and see a particularly beautiful sunset but my eyes would always fill with tears at the sight and at the thought of what I had had to give up. I dared not travel on the roads Dickie used to take me on. They held too many memories. I think I grew quieter. Marlene and

Jimmy were often by my side, trying to comfort me. But my heart felt dead inside.

'You seldom laugh now, Aviü,' my father scolded me one day. But his eyes were full of love and concern, conveying in his own sparse way what he held back from saying. How painful it was to laugh now. How much easier it was to cry than to make the effort to laugh.

February 1950

My girls were growing rapidly. When they were ready to go to the Mission School, I spoke to Sam about getting some skills so I could get a job and support them. Soon, I was on my way to fulfill an old dream – to become a qualified nurse. Of the colleges I had applied to, the most attractive seemed to be the Christian Medical College in Ludhiana. It was one of the best hospitals in India at the time. The course was three years of general nursing and one year of midwifery. That meant I would have to be away from my girls and my family for four long years. It was heartbreaking to leave my girls but I had to make that decision. I needed to get the training so I could get a good job and support my family.

On my first night at the college hostel, I could not sleep. How I missed home. The days were gruelling because there was so much to do, so I rarely had the time to think of my own troubles. But when night came, I was struck again by the thought that I would not be able to go home for a long time. Most nights my pillow would be soaked through with tears.

Our sister superintendent was a gentle, elderly woman. She took me under her wing and often called me to her office to talk to me and pray for me. I can never forget her kindness. It was her support that helped me to work persistently at my studies. I struggled more than my friends since I had had a much longer break from studying.

Though the next three years were very lonely, I was able to go home twice on short visits to see my girls and be with my parents and brother and sisters. On my first trip, I tried to stay home as much as possible so I could spend time with them. My studies also became easier after a while. Slowly, I gained more skills and knowledge and I became more interested in what I was studying. I was now eager to learn even more.

When I was in my final year of nursing, I came across an advertisement inviting young women to join the military nursing services. I was very taken by it and sent off my application at once. During the war, some of the older girls had joined the nursing services. I had dearly wanted to go then but I was underage and my application had been rejected. Now my application was accepted and shortly after, I was asked to appear for the interview in New Delhi.

When the sister superintendent heard that I had been called for the interview she was very disappointed. She called me to her office and pleaded with me to finish my course. I felt bad that I had upset her and I withdrew my application. She had been very caring and had looked after me and I did not want to disappoint her. After a few weeks, she had a stroke and had to leave India. Her departure broke many hearts in the hospital as she was dearly loved by all of us.

In a few months, my final exams were over and I was free to leave Ludhiana. I went to Delhi to do a one-year course in obstetrics. In Delhi, I felt less lonely and less homesick because there were a few other students from home and we frequently met at church. At St Stephen's Hospital, where I was studying for my course, the sister superintendent was warm and kind. Our tutor and our civil medical officer were also patient with us and made us feel at home. Life was made much more pleasant because of their kindness. I began to eat properly again and felt happier in Delhi. The unbearable homesickness I had suffered in Ludhiana slowly passed.

February 1952

I found many things changed when I went home on my second holiday. The girls were much bigger than I remembered them. They had already started going to school. Aneiü looked after them at home, tutoring them in their studies and making them new dresses when they outgrew their old ones. Many of my friends had also got married.

The day after I arrived, Jimmy came to see me. I was so pleased to meet him. He filled me in on all his news.

'Can you believe? Marlene's got married and moved away,' he said.

'No! Really, Jimmy? How old is she now?'

'About nineteen,' he replied. 'She lives in Assam now with her husband and baby.'

I was rather stunned by this news. Jimmy looked older but he was still his friendly self. He had been like a younger brother to me, like family, so we were always relaxed and comfortable with each other. He said he was trying to make a living and settle down.

Seeing Jimmy brought back memories, both sweet and bitter. We spent the entire afternoon together, talking about the old days and our shared experiences. He still lived in his father's house, adjoining our upper garden. Jimmy said he would get married as soon as he got a job. I was happy for him.

I knew Jimmy had the mettle to make something of himself. He had proved this when we were running from the Japanese in the woods. I told him I hoped things would work out for him. Jimmy was the sort of person who deserved happiness in life.

But the best part of my short holiday was to be able to be with my girls again. They showed me their schoolwork, all the alphabets and words they had learnt to write. They drew a lot, pictures of funny animals and hills and trees. I took some of their drawings back with me to paste on my bedroom walls.

I had to go back to Delhi after eight days because I was scheduled to sit for my final examinations. I gave the exams and completed my course, passing with an A grade. I was thrilled for more than one reason. Finally, I could go home and be with my loved ones.

It was wonderful to return, having passed my exams well. For the next few years, I spent time at home with my girls, trying to make up for all the years we had been parted. They went to school at the Mission School, my old school, and we lived with my parents in our old house.

April 1956

Sam had been working as supervisor of the Commonwealth War Graves for some years. He asked me to apply for a job in the Assam Oil Company in Digboi. My application was accepted and I had to report for duty immediately. We agreed that I would start work and find some way of getting the girls to join me later.

I joined the Digboi Assam Oil Company hospital in January 1956 as a member of their senior staff. Digboi was a beautiful oil town. I felt at peace there. I enjoyed working in the Company, which had an international atmosphere with officers of different nationalities. The oil fields were surrounded by tea plantations and you had to drive past miles of green tea gardens just before you reached Digboi. There were many families living in the oil town and it was a cozy and friendly place. The hospital had high standards. All the rooms were very clean and we were expected to maintain these standards. I thoroughly enjoyed my work and living in the town.

The social lives of the workers at the hospital revolved around the Oil Company Club which showed Hollywood movies every Wednesday and Sunday. There was a movie hall in the town as well and the tea planters' club also showed movies. Life on the plantations would have been very lonely without our club. Various social events like dinners, dances, swimming galas and tennis and golf matches were organized for both young and old. There was always some event or the other happening at the club and everyone participated eagerly, the employees' families driving long distances to participate in the annual club meets.

Sam's job with the Commonwealth War Graves Commission kept him very busy. Part of his job was to tour the war graves in the north-east. The tours brought him to Digboi on occasion. I looked forward to his visits for he would bring me letters and news from home.

I lived in a big Chang bungalow, a spacious house made of wood and bamboo with a thatched roof that made the house very comfortable because it kept the heat out and let the rooms remain cool during the hot Assam summers. I shared this house with three other senior sisters and we each had our own room and shared a lounge, kitchen and dining room. In the room next to mine was Sister Jagathambal, an elderly army sister.

I was trying to earn enough money to rent a house of my own and bring my girls to Assam to live with me. But it would be a long time before that could happen. I wrote to them as often as I could and they sent back letters with their little drawings, warming my heart and giving me strength each day.

One afternoon, Sister Jagathambal said to me, 'You must be lonely, my dear, as there are not many young people of your age around here. I happen to know a nice family with grown-up daughters; I will introduce you to them next Sunday.'

The family she spoke of did not live too far from us. The next Sunday, she took me to meet Mr and Mrs Theodore O'Leary and their three daughters, Colleen, Doreen and Barbara, and two sons, Patrick and William.

Mr O'Leary was an officer in the Assam Oil Company's engineering department. He used to work for the Burma Oil Company but during the war all foreign workers were evacuated from Burma. Mr O'Leary was sent to India where he joined the army as a captain in the Royal Engineers. His family was sent to live in Bombay. After the war, he and a few of his friends, who had also come from Burma, joined the Assam Oil Company in Digboi and stayed on in India.

The O'Leary sisters were lively girls, a little younger than me. Barbara was much younger and Doreen and Colleen were closer to my age. We began to go to movies together and I was invited to their home a few times. They seemed to like me a lot, and I found them good company, too. Their older brother Patrick was shy and we did not speak much to each other, while young Willy was very friendly and liked to be with us girls.

September 1956

One afternoon, when I had just come home after finishing duty, the caretaker of our bungalow announced that I had a visitor. I wondered who it could be. I thought it must be one of the girls I had recently met at the club. To my surprise, it was Patrick O'Leary. He seemed ill at ease and I thought he may have come on an errand for his mother or one of his sisters.

Instead, he looked at me and asked, 'Mari, you wouldn't like to go see a movie with me, would you?'

I was quite unprepared for this and when I hesitated, he quickly added, 'You needn't go if you don't want to.'

'Oh no, I would love to go.'

So we went to our first movie show; it was a Hindi movie.

We met again. The first few times we drank tea at the small hotels in town and spent hours together, just talking. Eventually, he began to come regularly to spend time with me after he got off work. Patrick, or Pat, as he was called by those close to him, had been working at the Assam Oil

Company for some time now. As we grew closer, I felt my admiration for him grow.

'I'm a man still trying to piece together his life, Mari,' he said one day. He told me how much it hurt him to be separated from his loved ones by the war. He had been twenty-three when he came to India and began to work and he was still grieving over being parted from his grandmother, whom they had been forced to leave behind in Burma.

Over our teas and movies, we soon fell in love and after a few months, Pat asked me to marry him. I was more cautious this time. I was not sure Pat was ready to be a father to my two girls. But he was wonderfully patient with me. He held me tenderly when I told him about Vic and Dickie and he told me, 'You have been through so much already. No one deserves as much pain as you have got from life. Please give me the chance to make you happy. I want to open a new chapter in your life.'

We spent more time together after that, getting to know each other better. We began to talk about getting married in the near future. I was truly happy for the first time in years. It was 1956. Ten years since Dickie and I had parted. I had long given up hope of being reunited with Dickie. But my love for him had remained, like a dull and constant ache. I thought of Vic differently, with gratitude and sorrow. I would always remember how much Vic had loved me. Yet fate had had its own way with us.

Once again, a truly wonderful man was offering me his love and devotion. I didn't want to refuse his offer. At the same time, he would need to meet my family and seek their approval. Most importantly, how would my girls feel? And Sam and Father and Mother? I did not want to marry against their wishes.

So much had happened in our family in the last ten years. Sam and his wife were now parents to five children. Zhabu had finished her nursing training and had been working for a few years. She was married now and had four children. She had coped well with motherhood and a career. She was working at the Kohima hospital so that her older children could go to school in Kohima. Aneiü had finished her education in Calcutta, was married and had a son. With even Aneiü married and a mother too, it felt as though life was passing all of us by. Mother and Father had new responsibilities now.

Marion and Lily were grown up now and their places were being taken over by the younger grandchildren. Mother took care of the younger ones as patiently as she had taken care of my girls when they were smaller. The big house was rarely empty now. One of us was always moving in for some time before getting on with our lives. Right now, Aneiü and her husband Joshua had moved in along with their infant son.

I dearly loved my family and I knew nothing would please them more than to see me happily settled in life. I was also deeply aware that any major decision I took would have to include all of them.

October 1956

It was around this time that there was political unrest in Nagaland. Letters from home were full of the tense situation and about the Indian army's killing of many Nagas who were fighting for independence from India. The situation became so serious that after a few months my family wrote to say that they were travelling to Assam to live with me till the worst was over. I was earning well so I did not mind hosting them. In fact, I could send home money regularly now that I was well-paid.

Sam and I had discussed the idea of my girls coming to live with me in Digboi, but they didn't want to leave their friends and their school, and I didn't want to leave Pat and my job. I welcomed the arrival of my family members. I did not know just how grave the situation at home was but I welcomed the opportunity to have my girls and the rest of my family with me. Pat found a big house for them at Makum, a short drive from Digboi, and we impatiently awaited their arrival.

Soon they were here. Father and my girls and my sister Zhabu with four of her children, Nino, Guo, Seno and

Asono. Mother had refused to leave Kohima. It reminded me of the war, when she had stayed alone in our big house. She had fed the Johnnies. That was what the young British soldiers were called. They came up the hill and rested before they climbed on further to oust the Japanese embedded in the village.

'Things are really bad at home,' said Father seriously. 'The Mission School has been closed down and the army has occupied the school buildings. The girls haven't been to school for three weeks now.'

I thought of the rest of our relatives and those who had not been able to leave. Many had sought the safety of nearby states like Shillong but there were others who were not rich enough to do so. How comforted I was that my loved ones could come to me, and it made me grateful to God for my job and placement in a safe town.

At this time, Pat was based in another town. He had been transferred out to Naharkatiya, an oil town about twenty-two miles from Digboi. He drove out to Makum to meet my family on their arrival. All of them liked him and they got along well. That made me happy as I had grown close to Pat's family. It was good that Pat and my family could meet and get to know each other at last.

From time to time, we received letters and news of home from Sam. It was not hopeful at all. In fact, in his latest letter, Sam mentioned that the Indian army had moved into our house and was using all the lower rooms except Mother's bedroom and kitchen. No one could tell when the conflict would end. So we decided to send the children to study at the Little Flower School in Dibrugarh. Sam's daughter Aleü had already been studying there for a year. In the following term, the three older girls, Marion, Lily and

Zhabu's daughter Nino, were admitted and they stayed in the boarding school. It worked out well for me as I could now have my girls quite close to me.

After a few months, Sam wrote to tell us that things were now more stable in Kohima. Father and Zhabu and her two young sons and baby daughter left soon after. They dearly missed Mother and their friends and their home, so when they learnt that our house was no longer occupied by the army, they quickly began to pack their bags. I wanted them to stay longer but they had really been quite homesick. All I could do was to make them promise to come back if trouble should erupt again.

Things were far from all right when they went back home. But at least the terrible shootings had quietened down in Kohima. I could only imagine how difficult it must be to live at home. Vivid memories of the last war came back to me and I wondered if it was as bad as that or worse. I impatiently tore open letters from home, expecting to hear the worst, though they always wrote that they were fine.

On the short school holidays that the girls got, Pat and I took them to his oil camp in Naharkatiya. At first, they were shy with him but they were well-behaved young girls. After a few visits, they all seemed more comfortable with each other. When the girls had longer holidays in winter, they went home to Kohima. They were very close to Father and Mother and loved spending time with their grandparents.

With Pat at the new oil camp, it was becoming increasingly harder for us to meet. He would drive the long distance on weekends to come and see me. But the road from Naharkatiya to Digboi was a rough country road, winding through dark jungles a large part of the way. It was mainly used by oil trucks to move drilling equipment and transport workers. It was dust-smothered in the dry months and could become muddy and slushy in summer. Many nights when we were driving back, we saw tigers, leopards and deer. A few times, wild elephants had stood in the middle of the road, and all we could do was wait as quietly as possible for them to pass.

I loved Pat and I knew he cared for me dearly. I thought of the perils he faced in coming to see me. And each time he drove back I prayed very hard for him to reach camp safely.

At least Pat and my girls were now getting quite close. I could see that he was very fond of them and they of him. I was pleased about this. If we were to marry, he would have to be father to my two girls, and it was important to me that they got along well.

February 1957

I had been working at the Assam Oil Company Hospital for about a year. Now that I had earned some leave I planned a visit to my parents. So much had happened in this one year, good and bad. I wanted to remember only the good and forget the bad. Pat was the best thing that could have happened to me. We had taken things slowly because we wanted to be sure it would work out. And now we were both certain we wanted to get married and spend our lives together.

Some months ago, Pat had written a letter to Father to say that we had known each other for a year, and that he loved me and my two girls and wanted to marry me and take care of all three of us. Father had liked him a great deal when they met. I travelled home, eager to know what his answer would be to Pat's proposal. To my great joy, Father did not hesitate to give his approval to our marriage. He said he was sure Pat was a man he could trust.

I returned to Assam with the good news. In great excitement, Pat and I both took a month's leave and drove home. It was a very long drive in Pat's jeep which he had just

bought from a Catholic priest in Digboi. On the Dimapur–
Kohima road, army convoys reduced Pat's driving to a
crawl. We reached home very late at night but were warmly
welcomed by Sam and Bano, Zhabu and Aneiü and their
families. They had taken care of all the arrangements for
our wedding.

Pat and I were married in Kohima on 15 February 1957.
And though February is the cloudiest of winter months in
Nagaland, the sky that day was bright and blue. The church
was full of people. They were mostly people from my family,
but some of Pat's friends had made the long trip to Kohima.
They were all so happy for us. I wore a white ankle-length
dress and Pat looked extremely handsome in his navy blue
suit. Zhabu cut long-stemmed water lilies for my bouquet.
They lasted all day.

After the ceremony, we all gathered in the front garden
where chairs and tables had been set up. My sisters and
their friends had been busy for days, decorating the place,
and it was really quite beautiful with flowers and crepe
paper. The wedding cooks had prepared enough food to
feed two hundred guests. Joe, Aneiü's husband, was a good
singer and he sang a lot of songs at our wedding. As the
evening wore on, other people began to get up and sing too,
and some danced under the open skies.

In another three weeks, we were packing to return to Assam.
But Pat was enchanted by Kohima. In the fifties, Kohima
was a little town recovering from the ravages of war. Most
of the houses were newly-built wooden cottages with tin
roofs and pretty windows. There was a freshness about the
town and the small community of people. Everyone knew
everyone else, which made it a warm and friendly place.

The months of February and March were pleasant in our hills with the warmth slowly returning after a long winter and I could well understand Pat's fascination with Kohima. 'We are coming to live here when we retire,' he said firmly.

Kohima, with its shops and houses dotting the valley and the hill slopes, looked very pretty both by day and night. In late winter, it looked even prettier against scarlet sunsets and dark blue night skies and you could spend all night gazing at the stars. The political conflict in Kohima was evident with the massive presence of the Indian army, but people were still able to come together for celebration. Our wedding had been one of those rare excuses.

Pat had been infected by that spirit of camaraderie and joie de vivre that always appeared in our people in hard times, as though we were trying to defy our fates. He loved everything he saw and everyone he met. And they loved him back. He was at home in our large family and got on very well with Sam and Father and everyone else. I felt like I had finally come home for the first time in a long, long time.

We still had a few days' leave left when we returned to Digboi. But Pat had to return to Naharkatiya, and we were together only on weekends. It was even harder than before. During the week, Pat came to see me as often as he could. But it was strenuous for him to drive so far after a long day of hard work. I felt sorry for him because he would drive miles just to be with me for a few hours before driving back to an empty house.

Finally, I resigned from my job and we set up house in the oil town of Duliajan where Pat was posted next. It was a new oil town but very self-sufficient and well-structured with neatly planned roads and residential areas. There were flowering trees along the streets that gave some shade and made it lovely to go for walks. It was also completely flat, which was very new to me. And the work siren going off four times a day took some time to get used to. There was a hospital in the town and a few clubs for executives and their families. The Company had also built a golf course, tennis and badminton courts and swimming pools so that families had enough recreation. The executive bungalow that Pat and I lived in was spacious and there was a sprawling garden where I loved to sit.

Though it was a hard life for Pat, who had to work long hours, the perks were good compensation. He had greater responsibilities in this job and had to be on watch constantly to prevent accidents at the worksite. These were often gruesome and fatal. It was a demanding job but he was happy there. The nature of their work, with its many risks, brought the men closer than they probably would have in other jobs.

In our first years together, I was filled with wonder that I could be so happy once more. When the girls were back in boarding school I felt lonely in the afternoons when I was on my own but I learnt to be a stay-home wife, helping the servants cook the food that Pat liked and making a home for us. At such times, I thought of my past and felt it had not been me but another person who had gone through all those things.

Another lifetime.

1963–1968

On Pat's few leaves, we would travel to Kohima and spend time with Father and Mother and the rest of the family. Pat was now a favourite uncle among my nieces and nephews. They had overcome their initial shyness and would run to him to be picked up and thrown in the air. As for Pat, he was extremely fond of the children and played with them for hours. He always remembered to buy chocolates and sweets for them and was sad when we had to leave. We were trying to have children of our own but nothing seemed to be happening.

Pat's other great love was automobiles. He would buy old cars and jeeps and take them apart and work on them for days. The garage in our house was a greasy place full of what seemed to me a lot of junk metal. Pat refused to let me clear it.

'Please, Mari, I swear all the pieces of metal here are very valuable,' he would insist.

It continued to amaze me how clever he was at putting things together. On the days that he did not have to work, he made me flower stands and other decorative items. It was his way of showing me he loved me, so I stopped nagging him about the mess in the garage. He also liked to make chairs and other furniture in unusual designs.

Pat's father, Tim O'Leary, was much older now and he had retired from his job in the Assam Oil Company. In the mid-sixties, many of our friends moved away from Assam to Bangalore and Bombay and Pat's younger brothers and sisters migrated to Australia. We missed them, especially Pat's youngest brother Willy, who was closest to Pat. We promised to visit them in Australia. Now, there was just Pat and me and his parents left.

Tim worried us when he began to feel poorly for several weeks in a row. In the first week of Tim's sickness, I used to tease Pat, 'Now I know where you get your stubbornness from. Your father is the most stubborn patient I have ever come across.'

My mother-in-law and I nursed him but Tim hated staying in bed or drinking bland soup. He had always been active and he dreaded being bedridden. In his last days, he grew very weak and one grey afternoon, he passed on quietly.

Pat and I were quite shocked by this. Tim was barely seventy when he died. I tried hard to comfort my husband as he buried his father. It was a short funeral. Tim probably wouldn't have liked it any other way. Dear Pat, he was so withdrawn over the next few weeks. I let him deal with his loss in his own way.

The O'Leary men never showed much emotion. They were like most men of their generation, I suppose. The war had showed them how cruel life could be. Pat's parents' house was strangely silent after Tim's death, which was unusual because Tim had never been a talkative man when he was alive.

After Tim's death, we slowly moved on with our lives. Our girls had passed out of school and wanted to go to Poona's Spicer College. They were there for two years at the very rigidly structured Spicer Adventist College. Poona was a lovely sprawling city. The military cantonment was a big part of the old city. Pat and I went to visit them there a couple of times and they came home to us in the holidays.

Both girls were homesick as Poona was quite far from both Kohima and Assam. Thankfully, they passed with good grades. After Poona, the girls moved to Calcutta, Marion to complete her Honours in English at Scottish College and Lily to study political science. It was lovely when they came to spend holidays with us.

Marion graduated after two years and went home to Kohima to look after Mother and Father. How amazing this reversal of roles was. Marion began teaching at the Baptist English School in Kohima. In addition, she tutored her young cousins who lived with their grandparents. As the oldest of the grandchildren, she was maternal and protective towards all her cousins and they loved to spend time in our old house. All the grandchildren could be found there at various times. Mother always cooked a big pot of food for everyone and the house would often be filled with visitors.

1971

In the beginning of 1969, Marion was being courted by the young Ronojoy Sircar, a tea planter in Assam. They spent many summer evenings in our home when she came on holiday, Rono playing the violin or serenading Marion with songs like 'Ten Guitars' with the heady scent of jasmine in the background. Marion was happy in the way we all wished for her to be happy. In those days of first love, I sometimes caught a glimpse of Vic in her. Like her father, she had beautiful eyes. Like her father, her joy showed through when she was happy.

In October 1970, Rono and Marion were married in Kohima with our blessings. Father was the minister at their wedding ceremony. That week, the white and pink chrysanthemums were in full bloom in Kohima. All the bridesmaids carried chrysanthemum bouquets and the pungent smell of the flowers remained in the house for a long time.

Rono worked at the Tara tea estate and Marion came to Assam to begin her new life as a married woman. We were very happy because they would live close to us now.

We were together every weekend; they would come over or we would go to spend the night with them. In these years, I was less lonely and Pat was a wonderful grandfather when Marion and Rono had two little girls.

The following year, letters from Father frequently mentioned that Mother was ailing. I went home twice to see her. She insisted she was fine. But I remembered how stubborn Mother could be. She looked frail. Still, she continued to busy herself around the house, pottering about in the garden.

Aneiü and my nieces, who were looking after her, assured me that they would let me know if Mother should get worse. But I returned to Duliajan with an anxious heart, feeling that my visit had not been of much use. The days dragged on with some letters from home. There was no mention of Mother's ill health for several months. But in April, my nephew Atuo gave us a sudden visit. I knew it could not be good.

'Is Mother dead?' I asked flatly.

'No, Anyie,' he replied, 'but she is quite weak. I came to fetch you and Marion.'

We travelled on the night train to Dimapur and drove to Kohima, reaching home at about ten-thirty in the morning. As I walked towards the unusually quiet house, I knew she had gone.

Mother had passed away an hour before we reached. They had already bathed her and laid her out in the parlour. I saw the silent groups of people flocking around our front yard dressed in black body-cloths. The house was so empty without Mother. We were all grieving. The occasions on which I had come home had always been happy ones. We were seeing death after a long time now and the darkness was unbearable.

We buried Mother in the church graveyard after the funeral. Pat managed to get some leave and rushed to Kohima to be with us. I did not want to leave for Duliajan too soon. Father was devastated by Mother's death and I realized how old he had become. Stooped over by his loss, Father was so different from the strong man of my youth and childhood. People came every day to pray with him and to keep us company.

All of us felt the loss of Mother and though it was expected, it still came as a great shock. I saw clearly now that it was Mother and not Father who had been the strong one in our family. She had quietly held us together, cared for our children when they were small and made sure we had hot food on the table at every meal.

I remembered how she had tried to comfort me after Vic's death. Every so often, she would make something nice for me to eat. We were not accustomed to hugging each other or showing affection but in times of grief, it was our way to offer food as a token of love. I had learned so much from her.

For days, we went through the tin trunks containing her dresses and the cloths she had woven as a younger woman. I came upon my sisters silently weeping when they found something she had made. We tried hard to hide our tears from the children. They had good memories of a loving grandmother. They should not have to share our grief.

1973

Father was never the same again. We all saw this. He would try hard to be cheerful but I detected a new note in his letters. He still wrote to me regularly in his clear, strong hand. However, it seemed more of an effort now and his letters were few and far between. He gave me news of the family and Kohima but the cheerfulness he used to inject into his letters seemed forced.

One day, his letter seemed to be particularly dark. He wrote: 'Aviü, life in Kohima has changed so much in the last few years. The people are not the same as I knew them in my youth. There are such terrible things happening at home, I do not like living here any more. We hear of things we never knew before. It makes me tired of life.'

I worried that Father might not be with us for too long. Lily had got a telephone installed in Father's house. On 8 November 1973, we got a phone call from Lily. Father had had a stroke. Marion and I left as soon as we could, travelling the same evening by train, just like we had two years earlier when Mother died. We reached Kohima the next day.

Father was in his room, bedridden. My once tall and strong father now had to be fed and bathed by others. I knew he must hate it. But he was too weak even to protest.

Father looked tired and lost. He was happy to see us but already seemed to be drifting away. He was quiet and asked for Mother once or twice. We hid our tears when he did that.

Father had been a good sportsman when he was younger, an avid football player who would never miss a match even when he was too old to play himself. His other love was gardening, and he liked nothing better than to work outdoors all day. If we couldn't find him in his study, we would send one of the children to the garden and he would be there, weeding a fruit tree or planting a new fruit. Now he did not look as though he had the strength to walk to the garden to look at his beloved trees. My sisters and I sat beside him in turns. We kept a constant vigil, wanting him to know how much we loved him.

On the night of the thirteenth, he was visibly weaker. I slept a little because the others insisted on it. Aneiü and Zhabu kept their night-long vigil. Sometimes they talked to him softly, and at other times they prayed with him. They also sang his favourite hymns in low voices. Father would drift into an uneasy sleep and then wake up to ask, 'Is it morning yet?'

At four in the morning, a very pale dawn lit the bedroom window.

'Apuo, it is morning,' said Zhabu to him. 'Will you have some tea?'

He sat up in bed to drink his tea. Then he lay back and said slowly, 'It is well with my soul.' He looked very peaceful as he said it, so peaceful that we were not prepared for his spirit quietly slipping away as he breathed his last. When we realized what had happened, we were overcome with grief. Our loud cries brought the men into the room.

At first, there were many details to be taken care of, relatives to be informed, the arrangements with the church for his funeral, as Father had been pastor in the village church for many years before he retired. After this was done, the finality of his death hit me. We were now orphaned in a sense. Mother and Father were both gone and I wept long and hard at the thought.

I suddenly felt old. Father had always been the decision-maker in our family and it was easy to tell him our problems and wait for his solution.

Every once in a while, Sam would consult me on details about the funeral service. If Father were here, he would have taken care of all this, I thought at one point, and felt foolish afterwards. How I missed him.

The church arranged a big funeral for him. We buried Father in a corner of the front yard of the house he had built with such love. We carefully laid the wreaths and flowers people had brought on the mound of red earth that was now his grave. A simple wooden cross bore his name and the date of his death.

1974

With Father's death, it was as though another chapter in my life had been closed. I felt both young and old. I felt the obligation to shoulder more responsibilities as the eldest daughter and yet, I felt vulnerable and not quite able to face up to such a task. At least Sam was there and since he was the oldest, I could still lean on him. Pat understood my loss and tried very hard to help me. He had rushed to Kohima to be at Father's funeral, trying in his gentle way to comfort every grieving member of the family.

The deaths of Father and Mother followed each other within a span of three years. Mother had died in 1971 and Father in 1973. Pat and I stayed back in Kohima a few more days. The house felt empty after the funeral. Father's books were still on their shelves. They had been his most prized possession. They were marked in red ink in places, and I remembered how he would call one of us to him and read out a spiritual truth or a story that had deeply moved him. He had continued to do the same with his grandchildren. He had spent much of his lifetime reading and educating himself and others.

As pastor of the Kohima village church, he sought out non-Christians relentlessly and wept when they rejected the gospel. Father and Mother took several young men into their home and sponsored their studies. These students usually came from interior areas like Pochury. The house adjoining our main house was never empty of lodgers.

Many of these protégées of our parents had managed to do well in their lives, getting an education and becoming a leader in their community. In a way, what our parents did with their lives seemed very small but it had far-reaching results; Father's keen eye, seeking out strangers in town whom he brought back home and gave shelter, and Mother's kitchen which was ever open to guests. The educated people in Father's time also opened their houses to the less fortunate and helped them get an education.

1975–1985

A year after Father's death, Lily married Smo Das. She was working for Air India now and the two of them were based in Calcutta. As an employee of Air India, Lily arranged for Pat and me to travel to the UK and the USA in 1980. We were able to visit Kent to see Pat's sister Colleen, who was in the last stages of cancer. We were happy to meet her; we knew we would probably never get another opportunity to see her. Thin and weakened by her disease, Colleen was a shadow of the vibrant girl I had known her to be.

After a week with Colleen, we travelled north to Stockport, Manchester and Consett, where many of our old friends had settled after retirement. It was at Stockport that we were introduced to a few of the World War II veterans – men who had fought in Burma, Imphal and Kohima. They were happy to meet me and we chatted for a long time about the Battle of Kohima. It seemed so far away and I marvelled that I had lived and loved through that battle. So much had happened since then. The men we met belonged to different regiments from Vic's, so I didn't really expect them to have known him.

Pat's old boss came to meet us in London. He was now

working in Scotland. He offered Pat a job in offshore drilling in the North Sea. We were both quite pleased with the offer. It would give us a chance to be close to his sister in the UK. On our return home, Pat put in his papers but a week later, we were deeply disappointed when the Company refused his resignation. They gave him a promotion instead.

In the next five years, Pat and I became increasingly busy with building our house in Kohima. Since Pat and I had always dreamed of spending our retirement years in Kohima, we decided to build a house on the forest lands that had belonged to Father. It was a secluded spot and the silence of the woods would be a nice change. Pat took early retirement in 1988 and we left Assam to settle down in our new house in Kohima.

Our life in Kohima was quieter. Pat continued to work on the house. I grew flowers and kept the house as neatly as I could. We both enjoyed living in the same town as my family, who had adopted Pat as one of their own. Sadly, Kohima in the late eighties was very different from the Kohima of the fifties. It was overpopulated and no longer peaceful. The conflict was still going on and it affected our daily lives. Nevertheless, we tried to live our new life as best as we could, grateful for its small blessings.

Lily and Smo moved to England in 1981 and we didn't see much of them for several years. Marion and her family left their tea garden home to be in Calcutta at Rono's new posting. They travelled to Kohima on holidays whenever they could. Pat and I had settled well into Kohima by now. Our house became a family gathering place. The porch overlooked the same woods where Mother, Marina, Zhabu and I had gathered firewood so many years ago. I often sat there in the evenings and listened to the cicadas sing.

1996–1997

1996 was a rather momentous year for us all. That was the year Lily met her father, Dickie, in the UK.

Lily and Smo were now well settled in the UK with their two children. In 1996, Dickie came to know that his daughter Lily was residing in England with her family. As soon as he found out he called her and then drove to her home. The two of them, father and daughter, stood for many moments, just holding each other.

When Lily phoned me with the news, I was stunned and struggled for some time to take in her news. Dickie alive and in touch with his daughter! I could hardly believe it. The rest of our family was just as astonished with this discovery. They all wondered how life had treated Dickie. They eagerly asked for more news. 'Will she send any photographs?' they wondered. Lily promised she would send photos of her father.

Lily was introduced to Dickie's family: Grant and Mandy, his children from his first wife, Pauline; Fiona and Nicholas, his children from his second wife, Susan. Dickie had married in 1949 after he returned to England.

I never met Dickie again though he had planned to revisit Kohima. Certainly the news that he was alive came as a big shock to me. But I had come to accept that we were not meant to be. After I met Pat, memories of Dickie had grown less painful until they faded into my past.

Two years after he found his daughter, Dickie died in a tragic car accident. I felt the loss for both of them. Yet I had to be grateful that they had actually been able to meet and express their feelings to one another. They had at least been able to spend time together, getting to know each other.

Their meeting seemed to me as unreal as my love story with Dickie. I never thought Dickie and I would hear from each other again. The second time he met Lily, he held her and told her softly, 'Lily, I loved your mother, I really loved her.' Then he was gone from her almost as suddenly as he had gone from me. Hearing about Dickie's death was sad, but not as hard as Vic's death had been to me. The many years between our parting had been a kind of death. Besides, I had found happiness with Pat and never considered any life apart from him again.

Back in Kohima, Pat and I felt old age creep up on us. My sisters' children came regularly to help me with the house, which had become too big for me to supervise. I had trouble with a stiff neck, which prevented me from doing all that I would have liked to. We stayed home more, learning to be content with each other's company and social visits. In a way, this was all we had ever wanted. To be able to live together in a house of our own. Quietly and peacefully. We needed nothing more. Life seemed to flow by like a lazy river, and for once everything seemed to be in place.

1998

One wintry morning in February 1998 Pat alarmed us all with a severe bleeding. He began to vomit blood after breakfast. He must have vomited half a bucket. When he revived, we rushed him to the hospital. In the Kohima hospital, they found a stomach ulcer that they suspected had caused the bleeding. However, another test in March diagnosed Pat with stomach cancer and he was quickly operated on at Woodlands Nursing Home in Calcutta. Poor Pat. Everything had happened so unexpectedly and now he was battling for dear life.

In the past, when we were getting our Kohima house constructed, we used to wait impatiently for the day we would finish with the work. We had hoped to enjoy Pat's retirement peacefully after that. This illness of his was such a blow. It seemed so unfair. Pat was only sixty-eight. He had never been seriously sick in all our days together. Only once had he been hospitalized to have a burst appendix removed. But he was well and out in a week. This time it was much more grave.

Pat was operated on a second time in May the same year.

The day after his operation, he had a million tubes sticking out of him. I had to be very careful getting round them, just to be able to hold his hand. He also had an infection from the air conditioning and coughed badly. It was very bad for his stitches. It hurt his lungs to cough and at the end of the day he was exhausted.

In his younger days, Pat was quite stubborn. If he had an ailment he would fight it hard. This time it was different. We felt he was giving up. He had lost his appetite and ate very little. Pat was dearly loved by my family and my nephews and nieces called or came to see him and prayed for him.

In June, he became restless and homesick for Kohima. We mentioned this to the doctors and asked if he could travel. They thought he was well enough to travel so we took a flight to Dimapur.

How happy he was to be back in Kohima even though it was to be a brief visit. We had a steady stream of visitors. On the first day, Pat walked feebly around the house. The next morning he stepped outside and looked at the new plants, the flowering honeysuckle in our garden and the summer trees. He ate properly and felt very well, so everyone thought he was on the way to recovery. But it lasted only a week. After that, he was listless and feverish. The Kohima doctor treated him but the fever stayed, so we called his doctor in Calcutta and were summoned back at once.

Another operation was performed but the doctor's face was drawn after it was over. 'I'm sorry,' he said, 'it's spread everywhere. There's nothing else I can do.'

It was like a death knell. Looking back I don't know how I ever got through the next months. All through our forty-two years together, Pat had always taken care of me. I had been dependent on him. Now I had to care for him and I felt a terrible helplessness at the sight of my strong husband lying in bed, needing to be urged to eat.

Many nights, he would be sleepless and then we would lie awake together, not talking, just quietly holding hands in the dark. On 28 October, death came quickly to my dear husband. We sang 'Amazing Grace' and tried to hide our tears as he sang feebly with us. And then, without a struggle, as gently as Father and Mother had slipped away, he was gone.

Our relatives in Kohima congregated to prepare our house to receive the body. The flight home was very different from the other flight in June. There was a great crowd of relatives to meet us and to take Pat home. We embraced in tears.

During the night-long vigil, there were so many mourners. At the funeral service, 'Oh Danny Boy' was one of the songs sung for him. It brought fresh tears for it reminded me how, in days past, Pat used to sing the same song in his rich baritone. It felt so right that we should be singing this Irish melody, which he had so loved, for the loving man who had come to make Kohima his home.

Pat was buried at the Khedi Church cemetery because he was a member of their church.

The loss of Pat was felt more deeply by the family than I had expected. The youngsters missed their dear uncle. Alone in our house in Kohima, I imagined he would come into the door, calling out 'Mari', or 'My girl' in his inimitable way. The house was so empty without Pat. I didn't want to think of how I would live my life without him. I lived one day at a time. In the days after his death, I would bring out the box of old photographs and go through them. Each picture brought back memories and each held a story that I recounted to my loved ones when they came to keep me company.

The children and grandchildren had their own good memories of Pat as a very loving uncle full of fun and life. They had all been a little shocked by Pat in his last days. From a very stout, strong man, he had suddenly become frail and a ghost of the man they had known all their lives. They were visibly gentler with him, trying to find something to do for him and hoping to express their love for him in little ways. I was grateful for that. And in spite of my pain, I was deeply grateful for the man who had loved me devotedly through our long married life, always trying to erase the losses I had suffered earlier.

Pat's grave faces east. In spring, it is covered with cornflowers and yellow daisies. I feel his spirit watching over me, hovering concernedly until it is my time to join him. Once again, I am alone. Sometimes I feel very lonely. I feel lonely even in a room full of people.

At times, the memories rush in unexpectedly and I feel overcome by them. There are days when they are too painful and I must dull my mind with the routine jobs of tending to the flowers or cleaning the house, but there is never enough to do. I love the time I spend with my grandchildren, with my nieces and nephews. When they gather round, they always want me to tell my story and so I have told it to different generations, one after another, and each eye is moist after the telling. 'Your story should be a book, Grandmother,' they say, and now it is.

Epilogue

It is very dark outside. Nearly two a.m. on the clock by my bed. I close the pages of my diary and lay it on the bedside table. I didn't realise how absorbed I had been in its pages. I have been reading it for the last eight hours. How is it possible that a life can be summed up in just eight hours? Everything I did, everything I thought, everything I saw, everyone I met. I remember things that happened fifty years ago as though they had happened yesterday. Yet I can't remember what I did last week. How strange memory can be.

As I switch off the night lamp, the cold air from my open window makes me shiver. I get up to close it and pull the curtains across. But not before looking out at the dark woods once more. Dawn will not come for another two hours and the hills in the horizon are outlined in sharp black silhouettes. An owl keeps hooting every few moments. That is the only sound for now. That, and the rasp of my breathing.

Kohima sleeps. A Kohima so different from the Kohima of my youth. It is rare to see it thus. Tranquil in the grip of sleep. I don't want to go to sleep now. I want to watch this stillness a little longer. It feels as though the past and the present are intermingling at this very minute. But only for a moment. And when I have closed the window, the past will have flown and the present will rush in and take over.

There. I have done it. Closed the windows. Slid my diary into the bottom drawer of my dressing table. But I can't seem to close the drawer shut. The edge of the diary sticks out and my eyes rest on it. I suppose it will always be like that. I suppose the past will always remain with me.

Acknowledgements

My thanks to the wonderful women who came together and transformed *Mari*, the book, from dream to reality. Jaya Bhattacharji Rose, Mita Kapur, Karthika and Neelini Sarkar, my excellent editor – we've come a long way, haven't we? Thank you, guys.

My family and friends, for supporting me through this journey, thank you for your gracious love.